THE DANGER GANG

AND THE ISLE
OF FERAL BEASTS!

Also by Stephen Bramucci

The Danger Gang and the Pirates of Borneo!

STEPHEN BRAMUCCI
ILLUSTRATED BY ARREE CHUNG

BLOOMSBURY
CHILDREN'S BOOKS
NEW YORK LONDON OXFORD NEW DELHI SYDNEY

BLOOMSBURY CHILDREN'S BOOKS
Bloomsbury Publishing Inc., part of Bloomsbury Publishing Plc
1385 Broadway, New York, NY 10018

BLOOMSBURY, BLOOMSBURY CHILDREN'S BOOKS, and the Diana logo
are trademarks of Bloomsbury Publishing Plc

First published in the United States of America in October 2018
by Bloomsbury Children's Books

Bloomsbury books may be purchased for business or promotional use.
For information on bulk purchases please contact Macmillan Corporate and
Premium Sales Department at specialmarkets@macmillan.com

Library of Congress Cataloging-in-Publication Data
Names: Bramucci, Stephen, author. | Chung, Arree, illustrator.
Title: The Danger Gang and the Isle of Feral Beasts! / by Stephen Bramucci ;
illustrated by Arree Chung.
Description: New York : Bloomsbury, 2018. | Sequel to: The Danger Gang and
the Pirates of Borneo!
Summary: Ronald Zupan, twelve; his friend Julianne Sato; and his butler, Jeeves,
face new dangers in the form of foxes, a sea monster, and an iceberg
hiding a Liars' Club lair when actor Jack Bricklayer is kidnapped.
Identifiers: LCCN 2017056225
ISBN 978-1-61963-694-1 (hardcover) • ISBN 978-1-61963-695-8 (e-book)
Subjects: | CYAC: Adventure and adventurers—Fiction. | Kidnapping—Fiction. |
Mistaken identity—Fiction. | Islands—Fiction. | Foxes—Fiction. | Sea monsters—Fiction.
Classification: LCC PZ7.1.B7513 Dai 2018 | DDC [Fic]—dc23
LC record available at https://lccn.loc.gov/2017056225

Book design by Jessie Gang and Jeanette Levy
Typeset by Westchester Publishing Services
Printed and bound in the U.S.A. by Berryville Graphics Inc., Berryville, Virginia
2 4 6 8 10 9 7 5 3 1

To find out more about our authors and books visit www.bloomsbury.com
and sign up for our newsletters.

For Julien River and Henry Alan—
two boys destined for lives of adventure

1

A Warm Welcome Back!

Hello again,

You probably know all about me after reading and re-reading my first thrilling adventure, *The Danger Gang and the Pirates of Borneo!* That brilliant escapade ended with your dashing narrator, Ronald Zupan, rescuing his beloved parents from the clutches of a foul-smelling cutthroat named Zeetan Z.

It's a tale as old as time: boy flies to Borneo, crash-lands airplane, befriends crazed hermit and his band of fruit-throwing orangutans, escapes tongueless giant, swims through underground tunnels filled with devilish traps, and returns victorious at the helm of a pirate ship.

Of course, I can't forget the important roles that my loyal butler, Jeeves, and dear friend Julianne Sato played in this quest.

FACT: It's literally impossible to forget, because they remind me all the time. Also, Julianne is watching over my shoulder as I write this.

If you'll recall, the last collection of our daring deeds featured notes from Jeeves at the end of each chapter. Sadly, instead of magnifying my dashing exploits, he mostly rambled on about the sport of cricket.

This time around, Julianne Sato—partner in grand

schemes, fencing expert, and eleven-year-old girl still watching over my shoulder—will be adding her thoughts. But instead of chiming in at the end of each chapter, she'll take up her pen only when she feels the need to highlight my dazzling bravery.

Nope. I'll actually cut in whenever Ronald misses something. Like forgetting to mention that it was me who figured out that Zeetan Z and his pirates lived in caves, or Jeeves who knocked out Gunting, the tongueless giant.

I'll probably also interrupt every time Ronald says things like "highlight my dazzling bravery" because that just sounds ridiculous.

More like *ridiculously accurate*! Now, let us plunge into the hair-raising action of my second magnificent tour de force: *The Danger Gang and the Isle of Feral Beasts!*

2

Dressed for Adventure!

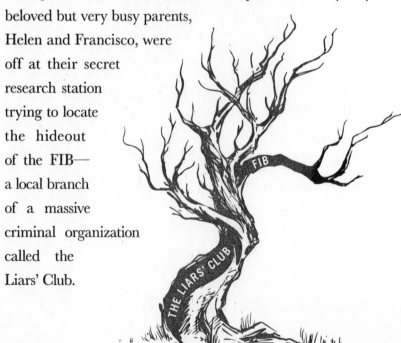

On a sticky Friday afternoon, near the end of summer, Julianne, Jeeves, and I were alone in the Zupan Manor. My very beloved but very busy parents, Helen and Francisco, were off at their secret research station trying to locate the hideout of the FIB— a local branch of a massive criminal organization called the Liars' Club.

Only weeks earlier, the FIB had ransacked our home while my parents were captives of the Liars' Club's leader, the infamous pirate Zeetan Z. The second we were back from Borneo, they began searching day and night for the FIB's hideout, hoping to recover artifacts stolen from our home. Their entire collection had been plundered—even the Brasher Doubloon, a rare coin worth millions. "The villains are toying with us," my father said, "like a black widow toys with its prey."

"They *must* be near here," my mother added, tapping her chin, ". . . or so we hear."

Ronald's dad has a lot of sayings that involve dangerous insects. His mom likes to use words that sound the same but mean different things.

It's sort of strange . . . but you get used to it.

Naturally, I was eager to help my parents track down our stolen treasures, but on this balmy night, Julianne had asked me to go with her to the movies.

FACT: A master adventurer never turns down the chance to help a friend.

Still, I can't say I was excited about the evening. The film was called *Buccaneers of the South Seas* and starred Jack Bricklayer, the hack actor who needed the Danger Gang to recover his replica pirate ship during our first adventure.

The name isn't Jack Bricklayer. It's Josh Brigand, which Ronald totally knows, even though he pretends he doesn't. Also, Josh is a fantastic actor with big blue eyes. "Piercing" blue is how I think people describe them. But Ronald is right about one thing: he definitely wasn't excited about going to the world premiere of Josh's movie. He was complaining nonstop.

"Seriously," I complained, stopping for a moment as Jeeves helped with my cufflinks, "why should I go to a party for this bumbling showman? He should be throwing a party for *us*."

Jeeves tugged on my sleeves and spoke in a low voice. "Ronald, you know that Julianne is excited about this. Josh wrote her idea for using trained orangutans right into the final scene of his movie."

"So why aren't *you* going?" I asked.

"Well . . . ," Jeeves said, brushing the lapels of my jacket and slicking down my hair with his fingers, "I'm just not the movie-going sort. Never have been. Instead, I'll be attending the ballet, across the street."

"But—"

"I'll pick you up the moment the film lets out, then we'll have an ice cream."

I would have argued more, but I've learned never to bicker when frozen dessert is on the line. Instead, I switched the subject to something that had been on my mind for weeks.

"Friends," I announced, "I've been thinking a lot about our next adventure."

Julianne was across the hall, getting ready in my mother's bathroom.

"And?" she called.

"We'll need our next daring escapade to be bigger, better, and more dazzling than our first."

Jeeves squeezed his eyes shut. "Oh dear."

"I thought we were trying to find my parents' ship?" Julianne asked.

Back in Borneo, I'd promised to help Julianne track down a long-lost music box aboard a sunken ship. It had wrecked when she was a baby, leaving her an orphan. As far as we knew, the ship was somewhere near Alejandro Selkirk Island, off the coast of Chile.

"We *are* going to find your parents' ship," I said. "That's stage one. But as long as we're south of the equator, I was thinking we could drop by the Peruvian Amazon. I've heard tales that the fabled city of El Dorado is hidden in that dense jungle."

"You can't be serious," Jeeves said.

"As serious as a bathtub full of vipers!" I answered.

Jeeves's eyes fluttered closed and he drew three slow, long breaths—a pet habit of his when I've proposed a spectacular idea.

"El Dorado," Julianne repeated from across the hall. "AKA: the Lost City of Gold."

"It won't be lost much longer!" I boomed.

I heard the bathroom door open and the sound of footsteps. I tried to face Julianne, but Jeeves was straightening my bow tie with one hand while holding my shoulders tight with the other.

"So, you want to recover my parents' sunken ship," she said, "then find the Lost City of Gold?"

As my adventure partner drew closer, I sniffed lemongrass soap—her telltale scent.

"Assuming that we get double-crossed by our jungle guide and have our underwater breathing hoses cut by scalawags, we should be able to avoid the second-adventure slump."

"The what?" Julianne asked.

I squirmed to get away from Jeeves, but he had me in an iron grip. Finally, I gave up and used my free hand to grab my adventure journal from my pocket, and pass it over my head to Julianne.

"Straight from Francisco Zupan," I said. "The page is marked!"

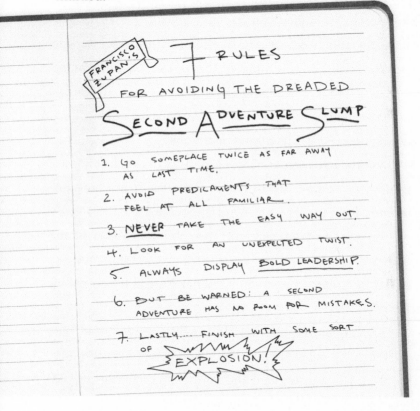

FRANCISCO ZUPAN'S

7 RULES

FOR AVOIDING THE DREADED

SECOND ADVENTURE SLUMP

1. GO SOMEPLACE TWICE AS FAR AWAY AS LAST TIME.
2. AVOID PREDICAMENTS THAT FEEL AT ALL FAMILIAR.
3. NEVER TAKE THE EASY WAY OUT.
4. LOOK FOR AN UNEXPECTED TWIST.
5. ALWAYS DISPLAY BOLD LEADERSHIP.
6. BUT BE WARNED: A SECOND ADVENTURE HAS NO ROOM FOR MISTAKES.
7. LASTLY.... FINISH WITH SOME SORT OF EXPLOSION!

"I'll tell you what . . ." Julianne said, reading down the list. "I'm thinking we should discover a rare species of Jurassic butterfly too. And there *must* be volcanoes down there, you know, for the explosion at the end."

"Sato, that's perfect!" I said.

"But . . ." She trailed off. "You remember that school starts in a week?"

My shoulders drooped and I felt my insides start to churn. "I thought we agreed not to say the 's' word."

My whole life, Helen and Francisco Zupan had left my education in the hands of professional tightrope walkers, tiger-wranglers, and, of course, Jeeves. But after losing our fortune when the FIB robbed our house, they'd decided to enroll me in the Bay City Public School System.

"It's not so bad," Julianne said. "We can carpool together. We might even be in the same homeroom."

"I'm used to instruction from experts of the ancient adventurous arts," I said, while Jeeves fussed with my bow tie. "Besides, Jeeves will be lonely if I'm not here to—"

"Oh, don't worry about me!" the good butler interjected. Our eyes met and he hesitated. "Erm . . . That's just to say, I'll be great. I mean 'good.' That is . . . I'll *manage* . . . somehow."

He finally released me, and I turned to face Julianne. She was wearing a yellow chiffon dress and bright blue slip-ons. Her black hair was braided and pinned up on her head, and she wore a pink hibiscus behind her left ear.

"You look every bit the movie star yourself, Julianne," Jeeves said.

He nudged me with all the grace of a drunken giraffe, and I added a dazzling compliment of my own.

"Yes . . . you . . . look like a bird—a bird of paradise or toucan. Not a vulture, because their heads are red and smooth from jamming their necks inside the body cavities of dead wildebeest. More like a—"

"You should stop now," Jeeves whispered over my shoulder.

"Indeed," I said, trying to loosen my collar. "So . . . we're off!"

Julianne glanced at my alarm clock. "We'd better hurry. It'll take us at least an hour to get to downtown Bay City in Jeeves's motorbike."

"Fear not," I told her. "We aren't taking that clanking pile of scrap iron."

"We're not?" Jeeves and Julianne asked at once.

"Friends," I said, "we're flying to the premiere in the Zupan family seaplane. It's waiting around the block at the duck pond."

Jeeves's face went pale. "Ronald, I'll remind you that not long ago you flew us to Borneo, crash-landed, and our plane blew to pieces in a fiery explosion."

Before I could argue this point, I spotted a flicker of movement by Jeeves's feet. I glanced down to discover my pet king cobra twining through the carpet.

"Jeeves, look out!" Julianne said.

It was too late. Jeeves groaned and rolled his eyes as the ferocious serpent shot forward and clamped its jaws right on the butler's kneecap.

3
Danger on All Sides!

"**R**onald, could you *please* get this blasted snake off me," Jeeves said, trying to pry the jaws of my beloved cobra, Carter, from his leg.

I unwound the snake and let him coil himself around my shoulder instead. "I'm sorry, Jeeves. But if Carter hadn't latched on to you at this exact moment, we might have forgotten to bring him."

The butler shook his head violently. "You are *not* bringing your pet cobra to the film premiere."

I looked to Julianne for help. She shrugged. "Maybe it's not the best idea. Even a defanged snake like Carter could scare people."

"Ha!" I scoffed. "How could a king cobra in a crowded movie theater *possibly* create problems?"

Jeeves adjusted his cummerbund. "Do you hear what you're saying? I feel like you don't always listen to the words that come out of your mouth."

"Sorry, Ronald," Julianne said. "I think it's a bad idea."

> FACT: The hardest part of having three people in the Danger Gang is getting outnumbered.

I consoled my pet by letting him bite my wrist.

"Oh *my*," Jeeves said, with a glance at his watch. "I'm afraid—"

"That the only way to make the premiere on time now is to fly in the seaplane!" I cheered, "Carter, you sly serpent, you've made this night better already!"

I ran off to set the cobra on my father's famous atlas, next to the radiator, then led my friends down the block to the local duck pond. We found the Zupan family seaplane tied up to the dock, with its chrome propeller glinting in the afternoon sun.

"Climb aboard," I said, "as Ronald Zupan once again proves that he can handle any aeronautic craft with the dexterous touch of a silver-tailed—"

The point is, Jeeves eventually agreed to let Ronald fly, since it was only a short trip at low altitude. We used the pond as a runway and I have to admit: everything went pretty smoothly.

Fifteen minutes later, we splashed down in Bay City Harbor, tied the plane to the wharf, and headed up the street toward the movie theater.

I was so excited I was practically skipping!

When we arrived at the theater, we saw a red carpet lined with a crowd of photographers, autograph hounds, and rabid fans.

"I'll be across the road at Ridgemont Hall," Jeeves said. "See you after."

He disappeared into the surging crowd and I swung to face Julianne. "Sato, the masses await."

I offered her my arm and she took it with a smile. Side by side we glided into the glow of floodlights and flashbulbs.

"Those are the kids who brought Brigand's ship back from Borneo!" someone yelled.

"You two," a photographer cried, "turn here!"

Julianne and I spun around, both smiling wide. All eyes were on us. It was too bad my parents couldn't be there to see it.

"What are your thoughts on *Buccaneers of the South Seas*?" a reporter called.

"Well," I said, striking another bold pose, "clearly there would be no movie if the Danger Gang hadn't—"

Halfway through my sentence, the whole crowd turned away to watch a stretch limousine glide up to the curb. Light from the popping flashbulbs bounced off its tinted windows.

"It's *him*!" someone yelled.

The door swung open and a man with a stubbly chin and aviator sunglasses exited the car. The crowd went wild—failing to realize that Sato and I were the *real* adventurers and the man they were gawking over was nothing more than a handsome, charming, internationally beloved actor.

"Josh, who designed your tuxedo?" one reporter yelled.

"Where's Isabella Montoya?" another called. "A little bird told me she didn't like the final movie!"

Julianne cupped her hands around her mouth. "Josh, we're down here!"

Brigand looked in our direction and his face lit up. "Julianne! Ronald!"

He strode toward us—scribbling autographs, hardly looking at what he was signing—then scooped Julianne up in a hug.

"Ronald," he said, clasping my hand and raising it high for the cameras, "so happy to see you! Why haven't you been coming for tea and cake at my estate with Julianne and Old Sato?"

Before I could answer, he was dragged off for more questions. I scowled at Julianne. "You and your grandfather go to tea and cake with Jimmy Blockhead?"

She leaned close. "It's *Josh. Brigand.* And yes, every Friday. He's been inviting you, too."

I frowned. "Then why is this the first I've heard of it?"

"Because you always say his name wrong," she said, "and you don't *like* him."

She had a solid point, but that didn't make it sting any less.

"I like *cake*, though!" I snapped.

Moments later, Brigand returned and whisked us inside. The noise of the crowd faded as we stepped through the glass doors. In the lobby, a concession girl carrying a tray loaded with candy, soda, and striped popcorn boxes rushed toward us.

"Popcorn? Cola? Peppermint Patties?" she asked.

"Thanks," Julianne said reaching for one of each.

The concession girl turned to me. I narrowed my eyes and gazed straight into the windows of her soul.

"Let me ask you a question. Who do you think is more impressive: an actor who *pretends* to be an adventurer, or a boy who defeats a wretched pirate while sword fighting on a pile of bat dung?"

Her only response was a confused stare.

"Let me phrase it another way," I said. "Imagine you were going to ask someone for an autograph—"

Julianne elbowed me in the ribs—a technique for getting my attention that she relies on a little *too* often.

"Ronald," she said, dragging me away, "you're acting *particularly* weird tonight."

"I was just making small talk," I replied. "I wanted to see if we had similar interests."

"No," Julianne said as we followed the buzzing crowd down the theater aisle, "you wanted her to say that you're more adventurous than Josh."

I shrugged. "Well . . . *that* would be a similar interest."

Brigand sat down in the middle seat of the middle row. There was a spot reserved for Julianne on his left and one for me on his right.

"This is so exciting!" Julianne gushed as we sidestepped to our seats. "Josh, you must be thrilled!"

"And a pinch nervous," the movie star confessed, rubbing his hands together. "I put everything into this film. What if the crowd doesn't laugh in the funny parts or cry in the sad parts, or fall in love with the brave hero?"

"Very possible," I said, only half listening. "They could hate it . . . or worse yet, ignore it all together."

Julianne shot me a look. "Don't listen to him, Josh. I'm sure it's great. And I'm so flattered you added my idea about the fruit-throwing orangutans!"

The actor chewed his lip silently. A few seconds later, the lights dimmed and the red velvet curtains pulled back to reveal a wide shot of a jungle.

Everyone in the theater clapped as giant letters flashed across the screen:

CAPSTONE PICTURES PRESENTS
BUCCANEERS OF THE SOUTH SEAS

Written by . . . JOSH BRIGAND
Directed by . . . JOSH BRIGAND
Starring . . . JOSH BRIGAND

The jungle slowly dissolved into a man standing at the helm of a ship.

"So we meet again, Cannonball Island," said the man on-screen (who was also the man sitting beside me).

The camera pulled back to reveal a parrot pacing on a nearby perch. The captain rubbed his chin and gazed into the distance.

"The last time I saw your shores I left a piece of my heart behind."

The parrot squawked. "*Akkk*—Princess Esmeralda—*Gaaak*."

"It's *Queen* Esmeralda now," the man corrected. "The rose of my heart's garden. The diamond of my eye."

"Sounds painful," I muttered.

"*Shhhhhh*," Julianne hissed.

Brigand sat with his fingers gripping his knees, leaning forward, mouthing every word. I could pretty quickly deduce that I'd need sustenance to power through this drivel. I reached across the actor for some popcorn, but Julianne swatted my hand away.

"How long is this movie?" I asked.

"Capstone wanted me to cut it," Brigand said in a hushed voice. "But I stayed true to my creative vision."

"Meaning?"

"It's three and a half hours."

I sunk in my seat. On-screen, the swashbuckler and his parrot recited a love poem together.

FACT: It was going to be a long night.

4

Mistaken Identity!

Before Ronald even gets into his thoughts on *Buccaneers of the South Seas*, let me just come right out and say: it could have been better.

Okay, fine. It stunk.

Watching Josh talk to a parrot for the first hour was . . . slow. Then there were chase scenes and swordfights, but it was all just sort of a blur.

I'd been excited to see the actress playing Queen Esmeralda, because I read in a newspaper that she did her own stunts, but all those parts must have been cut. Instead, she just sort of *appeared* at the very end and I hate it when characters just show up like that.

For Josh's sake, I hoped other people would love his movie, but by the time the credits rolled, the theater was half-empty. I jumped up to give a standing ovation as the lights hummed to life.

Julianne's clapping jolted me awake. I shook out my stiff legs and looked at the movie star seated beside me. His skin was slightly green, and his teeth didn't gleam quite as white as usual.

"What's the matter, Brickman?" I asked.

"They hated it," the actor cried. "My heart and soul are in every frame of that movie, and they *hated* it!"

I gave him the sort of skeptical look Jeeves gave me, back when I tried to dig a secret tunnel under his bedroom.

"Your heart and soul are in *every* frame?" I asked. "Even the scene where the drunken buccaneer confused a sea cow with a mermaid?"

"It was supposed to be funny! Didn't you think it was funny?"

I was saved by a skinny teenager in a crimson uniform at the end of our row.

"Excuse me," he called, "can I ask a favor?"

Brigand's face softened a little. "What can I get you, young fellow? An autograph for your favorite chum? A publicity photo signed to your sweetheart?"

The theater employee looked away, scuffing his toe against the carpet. "Oh . . . I was just going to . . . I have to sweep this row."

The actor's whole body sagged and he started trudging up the aisle and out of the theater. The crowd of photographers was long gone. So were the fans and the studio executives.

We neared the glass doors of the theater, when a voice came from behind.

"MISTER BRIGAND! MISTER BRIG*AND*!" It was the chirpy candy girl we'd seen before the show. She was holding a silver platter and rushing toward us. "I was supposed to give you this when the movie let out!"

We all looked down at the platter:

BEST ACTOR, WRITER,
and **DIRECTOR AWARD**
Presented by
the Guild of Actors and Show People

"Look!" Julianne said. "An award from GASP! That should cheer you up!"

The actor hung his head, running a finger across the engraved lettering. "I . . . I sort of . . . *invented* the Guild of Actors and Show People. To build buzz."

FACT: Creating a fake organization just to impress people sounded like my type of idea.

"Well done," I said, stroking my upper lip. "Maybe I should start a club and name myself *Adventurer of the Year*. Or better yet, *Adventurer of the Decade!*"

Julianne rolled her eyes and spun away. "Let's just get some ice cream."

Josh trudged toward the street holding his platter. I could see that the concert hall across the street had closed up already, but there was a light on in the tea shop two doors down.

I started toward it. "I'll get Jeeves!"

"Wait, I want to talk to you again really quick," Julianne said. "Josh, you okay?"

Brigand had plopped down in the middle of the red carpet and was using the silver award to inspect the lines around his eyes. Julianne pulled me back inside the theater lobby.

"Ronald," my adventure partner said, "could you be a little nicer to Josh? He's had a rough night."

I glanced sideways at her.

"And call him by his *real* name?"

"Fine," I said. "But you have to admit that movie was absolute—"

"LET GO OF ME, YOU BRUTE!"

It was Brigand's voice, echoing behind us. We turned to see him being dragged, kicking and screaming, off the curb by a gang of thugs in bandit masks. They shoved him into the back seat of a black sedan.

"STOP!" the actor yelled. *"HELP!"*

Julianne raced toward him, and I bounded after her. The driver's side window of the sedan rolled down, revealing a familiar-looking man with a square jaw and overgrown eyebrows. He held up a stun gun, crackling with electric pulses.

"Not another step, kiddos."

We skidded to a stop in the middle of the red carpet.

"Sorry, Ronald Zupan," he said in a flat, thudding voice, "we're kidnapping your beloved butler."

"That's not my beloved butler!" I yelled back. "That's just some world-famous movie star!"

"LET HIM GO!" Julianne yelled. "*JOSH!*"

The driver of the car glanced into the back seat. "Of course it's your butler. He has a tuxedo! And he's carrying a platter— probably for holding cocktails and appetizers!"

"My butler is British! . . . And *bald*!"

The villain glowered right at me, then sneered. I recognized those teeth immediately.

"I know you!" I said. "You're the FIB rogue with the terrible breath!"

"Breath? *What?*" the man said. "No! I'm Deadly Dirk Grimple—the one with the cool sunglasses!"

"The breath was more memorable," I said.

Dirk Grimple squeezed the stun gun again, and the blue electric pulses crackled with energy.

"See you later, Zupan," he said, "*if* you can find us!"

With that, he rolled up the tinted window and jammed on the gas. The car's wheels smoked and screeched as the devilish fiends raced away.

5

Miss-Taken Mistaken Identity!

Seconds after Grimple and his FIB goons sped away from the movie theater, vowing that I'd never see my beloved butler again, I saw my beloved butler again. He'd left the tea shop and was loping toward us.

"What's all the commotion?" Jeeves asked.

"The FIB kidnapped Josh Brigand!" Julianne said.

Jeeves tilted his head and frowned. "*Why?*"

"They thought he was you," I said.

The butler peered down the hill, toward Bay City Harbor. "And why would they want to kidnap *me?*"

"They *must* be headed to their secret hideout," Julianne said, pacing along the curb, popping her knuckles. "But even Helen and Francisco haven't been able to find it."

Jeeves nodded, still stunned.

"They drove toward the harbor," Julianne went on. "So they're probably traveling by boat." She looked over at me. "Hello? Any ideas? This is clearly a job for the Danger Gang."

"Or the police," Jeeves offered. "Police would be good."

I hesitated. "I . . . actually agree with Jeeves. I'm sure the Bay City police can—"

"You *what*?" Julianne yelled. "What are you talking about!"

I chewed my lower lip. "Well . . . If we rescue Josh, then *that* will be our second adventure. And we already solved a kidnapping. You saw my dad's list about the second-adventure slump. It's not supposed to feel familiar."

"I don't *care*," Julianne said, flagging down a taxicab that was idling down the block. "Josh needs us." She looked at Jeeves. "Can you talk sense into him . . . please!?"

The butler's face tightened as he stared down the street in the direction the villains had gone.

"Hurry!" Julianne yelled.

"Oh, blast it all," Jeeves said. "Ronald, I suppose we'd better go after Josh."

A yellow-and-green taxi rumbled to a halt, and my adventure partner dove inside. Jeeves motioned me to follow her.

I gaped at him. "But the second-adventure slum—"

"It's not your second adventure," he said, pushing me toward the open door. "It's just a . . . *side adventure*. Like in cricket, when the bowler causes a 'super over' in a test match after the seventh tea break and—"

"They're getting away!" Julianne cried, slapping the fake-leather seat.

"Side adventure, eh?" I asked, rubbing my chin as Jeeves guided me toward the open door. "Like it's still connected to the first one?"

"That's exactly it," Jeeves said. "Your parents go on them all the time, I promise."

I wavered, half in the car. "Seems like my parents could come up with a more dashing name. It could be called an 'Add-On Exploit' or—"

Jeeves gave me a final shove and we tumbled into the cab together.

"Follow that car!" Julianne yelled, pointing the cabby in the direction the FIB had gone.

"We're on a side adventure!" I added.

You. Have. Got. To. Be. Kidding. Me.
   Side adventure? Add-On Exploit? First of all, the whole idea is crazy. I could tell Jeeves was making it up. Second of all, if you had to come up with a better name, it should be a "Follow-Up Feat."

The cabdriver looked like the great-uncle of someone's great-uncle.

"What's that about a car?" he asked, digging a pinkie deep into his ear. "I don't see anyone."

"Because they're getting away!" Julianne said.

"But I can't see where they went to follow them."

"To the harbor! The harbor, good man!" I called.

The cabdriver ground his gears twice before we finally sputtered off down the road.

FACT: The Danger Gang was on the case!

I would have been even madder at Ronald for all the second-adventure slump talk, but I was distracted by something. A small red coupe was creeping down the road in our direction.

It struck me as strange. A tiny voice in the back of my brain wondered, "Why does that car have its lights off?" When our taxi finally started moving, I looked back again.

Sure enough, the car was following us.

6

Out to Sea!

By the time we puttered down to the Bay City wharf, there was no sign of Josh Brigand or the rogues who kidnapped him, just a few fishermen loading wire crab traps onto a dingy-looking boat. Julianne, Jeeves, and I dove out of the taxi and bolted up to the men.

"Hello, rugged crabbers," I said. "Have you seen any suspicious activity this evening?"

"Like what?" a rough-looking man grunted. He flung a crab trap onto a pile and mopped his oily face with his sleeve. His fingers were thick and blunt, and his nose looked like a tulip bulb.

"Like a movie star getting kidnapped against his will," Julianne said. "Kicking and screaming as a crew of villains dragged him away."

The crabber sized up my adventure partner and offered a slow nod. "Yep. We saw something like that."

"Tell us everything," I said.

"It was just what the girl described," the crabber replied. "A man kicking and screaming with a bunch of other people dragging him along."

"And did you note where they went?" Jeeves asked.

The man blinked a few times. "Due west. Straight toward the horizon."

We all looked to the west. It was dark and we couldn't see anything. Then the blue-black sky was torn in half by a jagged lightning bolt.

"Summer storm brewing," another crabber piped up. "Wind whipping up a gale."

The lead fisherman spun to grab another crab trap, but Julianne stepped in front of him. "Anything *else* you remember?"

The man wet his cracked lips. Between the fishermen and the taxi driver, none of the odd characters we'd met on this side adventure seemed to move any faster than a sloth after a sleeping pill.

"They were all in a boat," he said, "but then someone saw a red seaplane tied up and called to the others. There was arguing. Finally, the one who was kicking and screaming got dragged over to the plane. Half the crew flew, and the other half sped away in the boat."

My stomach sank. I turned to look down the wharf, but there was no need.

FACT: Through some bit of clever trickery, the scoundrels had stolen our seaplane.

Do you get to call it "clever trickery" when the keys were left in the ignition? I don't think so. Ronald even said, "That's Francisco and Helen's plane. No one would dare to touch it unless they were thieves, villains, or cheats."

But guess what? The men who took Josh were all three, and now we had no way to chase them.

I turned back to the lead fisherman. He'd started tying slick strands of fish gut into the traps.

"Sir," I said, "we're going to need to commandeer this vessel."

"What?"

"We'd like to borrow your boat," Jeeves said.

All the crabbers stiffened and looked toward the bow. We turned to see a square shack, built right onto the deck. There was one smoky window facing our direction, and through it we could spy the light of a flickering lantern.

"If you want the boat," the lead crabber said, "you'll have to talk to Cap."

7

Jeeves's Gambit!

Thunder crashed in the distance as Julianne, Jeeves, and I crossed the deck. When we reached the cabin door, I glanced back at the crabbers—they were slack-jawed, staring at us.

I raised my hand to knock when a voice cut through the night.

"*What. Is. It?*"

The voice clearly belonged to a woman, and it punched a hole in the thick air.

"Ahoy, dear captain," I called, "we're the Danger Gang, and we need a—"

"*I don't do favors!*"

I glanced at Julianne for some help.

"A band of criminals just kidnapped the movie star Josh Brigand," she called through the door. "Your crew says they—"

"*Don't. Do. Favors!*" the voice repeated. Then, after a pause, the woman added. "Brigand? He made that movie five years back, *Cannonade on the Spanish Main*, right?"

Julianne saw her chance. "Yes! And tonight he was abducted after the premiere of his newest movie. If you help us rescue him, he'd probably—"

"*Cannonade on the Spanish Main* was trash!" the captain shouted. "He made us seafaring folk look like fools!"

Another jagged streak of lightning lit the sky. The thunder rattled the walls of the cabin, and the first drops of rain splatted down on us.

Jeeves peered through the smoky window, his nose practically touching the pane. Inside was a small table with a chessboard. It looked like someone had paused midgame!

"A storm is coming and we have a lot of sea to cover!" the captain bellowed. "You three need to—"

"You're working on the Budapest Gambit," Jeeves interrupted.

Julianne and I stared at him. Behind us, one of the crabbers gasped.

There was an electric pause, then the good butler spoke again. "I'd say it's time to bring out your rook."

"Who said that?" the captain demanded. Her voice had shifted a little; it carried a hint of curiosity.

The rain flattened Jeeves's last wisps of hair. "My name is Tom Halladay."

"Play chess, Halladay?"

"My employers prefer Scorpion Poker," Jeeves said, "but chess is my first love. I'm familiar with the Budapest Gambit."

There was another pause.

"Come in," the captain said in a low voice. "*Alone.*"

Jeeves shrugged at us and slowly creaked open the door. He slipped inside, leaving Julianne and me to twiddle our thumbs in the rain. We stood quietly, straining to hear what was being said in the captain's cabin.

"Just like Jiffy Bristlebrush to get kidnapped at his own movie premiere," I finally grumbled.

Julianne glared at me. "Why in the *world* would you leave the keys in the seaplane?"

I looked down at my tuxedo shoes, embarrassed. "I . . . don't like having things in my pockets," I mumbled.

Julianne grunted in disgust. With nothing else to do, I turned to look at the crew of crabbers. I wanted to be sure they were in prime condition for our side adventure.

FACT: They were *not* in prime condition.

Finally, the door opened behind us. I turned to see Jeeves wearing a strange half grin.

"She's going to help us," he said. "*If* I play chess with her during the voyage."

The news made my adventurer's spirit surge.

"You heard him," I announced to the crew. "Cast off the bow lines! Man the sweeps!"

The men stared at me blankly. Finally one of them spoke. "Kid, this boat just has a motor."

I sighed. Clearly the crabbing vessel was full of adventure novices.

The crabbers trudged across the decks like they were sleepwalking. Each one was slower than the next.

"Sorry, Sato," Ronald said, "I don't think anyone could get these louts moving."

Just then, an intercom squealed and the

captain came on. She didn't say anything, she simply cleared her throat.

It was more than enough. Instantly the whole crew flew into action. In seconds we were headed west.

"That did the trick," Julianne said.

Another giant flash of lightning streaked across the horizon and we glimpsed the silhouette of our stolen seaplane disappearing into a cloudbank. There was no choice but to follow it, right into the eye of the storm.

"Ronald Zupan?" the captain called over the intercom. Everyone froze.

"Yes?" I answered.

"Someone's asking for you on the radio."

8
Archenemy on the Airwaves!

Jeeves pushed open the door and we stepped inside the captain's cabin. The room was dark and cramped, with the chessboard and a hammock off to one side and a desk spread with charts on the other. Everything was bolted down or tied together with wire.

The front of the cabin had a wide glass window facing out on the churning ocean. The captain stood with her back to us, steering the boat with one hand while she fiddled with a radio dial.

"I swear," she said, without turning around, "I just had the signal."

She was every bit as tall as Jeeves. Her black hair was braided and she wore it pinned up on her head.

"Delenda Jean-Baptiste," she said. "Great-granddaughter of the famous New Orleans riverboat pirate. Crew calls me Cap."

She glanced down at us. Her eyes were bright and I quickly deduced that she was no one to trifle with.

"I'm Ronald Zupan," I said, "and this is my partner in grand adventures and dazzling schemes, Julianne Sato. You already met Jeeves."

The captain narrowed her eyes at the tallest of our trio. "You told me your name was Tom. Were you lying?"

The butler shook his head. "Jeeves is sort of a . . . *nickname*. Only Ronald and Julianne call me that."

The captain eyed him for what seemed like ages. "I like Tom better."

"Me too," Jeeves said.

The radio sputtered and popped, and Delenda reached down to try to find the signal. Someone was talking, but it was too fuzzy to understand.

"Grab this." She motioned for Julianne to take the huge silver steering wheel.

We were outside the protection of the harbor now and the bow of the boat reared up as we crested a wave, then slammed down again with a terrible groan. Julianne had to wrestle the wheel to keep us pointed straight. Rain slatted against the window, and water washed across the decks.

Delenda tried for another minute to tune the radio, then

gave the whole system a rattling slap. There was a loud, fuzzy whine, and a man's voice crackled across the airwaves.

"Ronald Zupan," he snarled, "are you brave enough to answer?"

Whoever it was sounded as sinister as a Peruvian panther. Delenda pushed the radio receiver toward me. I took it and pressed the button to talk.

"I'm Ronald Zupan," I said. "Only son of Helen and Francisco Zupan, founding member of the—"

"Shut up," the man hissed. "I am your archenemy."

"Zeetan Z?" I asked.

"No!" the man said. "I'm far more dangerous than that bully. I'm the leader of the FIB—the most feared man in Bay City!"

The radio whined and squealed.

"What's your name?" I asked.

"Earlier tonight I sent my men to capture your beloved butler," the voice said. "Now *you* have to rescue him, it's part of my master plan."

Jeeves reached for the receiver. "Sorry to disappoint," he said, "but *I'm* Ronald's butler. The fellow you captured was a movie star by the name of Josh Brigand."

We could hear the scalawag slam a hand or foot against something hard, then he gave a long, pained cry. After a few moments of silence he spoke again, through gritted teeth. "That mix-up was less than ideal, but no matter. The actor

will do. He's a friend of yours and his life depends on you now."

I took back the receiver. "First of all, I wouldn't call him a friend." Julianne glared at me. "And second of all, the Danger Gang is coming to find you as we speak. We'll rescue Josh Brigand and take back my family's stolen artifacts. Including the rare Brasher Doubloon."

"I don't think so," the voice said. "Your parents have been trying to find those artifacts for weeks. The trail is ice cold. Just wait until your new archenemy—"

I snatched the receiver from Ronald and pressed the button to talk.

"Why is *Ronald* your archenemy?" I asked. "I'm a member of the Danger Gang too!"

"Who is this?" the voice said.

"Julianne Sato, fencing champion of Bay City! Ring a bell?"

"Zupan's assistant? The orphan. Yes, the assistant to my archenemy is also *my* enemy."

I could literally feel my whole face getting hot. "We're *partners*," I said between clenched teeth.

A wave smashed into the hull of the ship and it shuddered. It was hard to hold the radio and the wheel at the same time.

"Listen, whatever-your-name-is," the man spat. "If you were in Borneo, you're my enemy. But you don't know the tip of the iceberg about where I'm radioing from."

I squeezed the receiver so hard my knuckles turned white. "No, you listen to me. We're rescuing Josh, and whenever I find you, I swear, you will remember the name Juli—"

Before I could finish the radio buzzed and the line went dead. I slammed down the receiver and stared out the window into the storm.

Julianne's jaw muscles pulsed. I set my hand on her shoulder. "Clearly the FIB are horrible criminals."

She nodded her agreement.

Jeeves shivered. "Absolutely. That man said he was more frightening than Zeetan Z!"

"I meant horrible at *being* criminals," I said, as another whitecap broke across the decks. "Who kidnaps the wrong person?"

"Or doesn't know that I'm a founding member of the Danger Gang," Julianne added, still seething.

Another wave walloped us, and she fought to hold the wheel steady.

"Hopefully, they'll at least lead us someplace exotic," I said, "down old South America way, perhaps. Or Morocco."

"It's not Morocco," Delenda said, turning down the radio. "This signal catches people broadcasting for fifteen miles. Even less in weather like this. Wherever your new archenemy is hiding, it's close."

9

Capstone Island!

Delenda walked over to her desk and bent down to inspect a chart that was spread out on the table.

"I don't know where the FIB is," she said, "but that seaplane is headed to the harbor at Capstone Island. In this storm, it's the only safe place to land besides Bay City."

"Capstone?" Julianne asked. "Like Capstone Motion Pictures?"

Delenda nodded and took back over the wheel. "They once used it as a movie set. It's abandoned nowadays. All that's left is an old theater and a crumbling harbor."

"So you think the plane is going there?" I asked.

Delenda nodded as another long streak of lightning split the blue-black sky.

"Hmmm . . . ," Julianne muttered.

I knew this "hmmm." It was a sound my adventure

partner made when she had the sort of idea that I'd end up wishing I had first.

"What is it?" Jeeves asked.

The lantern flickered and the biggest wave yet dumped water over the bow.

Julianne grabbed my shoulder to brace herself. "An abandoned island that's close to Bay City? It sounds like the perfect hideout for a criminal gang. Right?"

"The FIB," Jeeves said, eyes widening.

"The man on the radio was probably calling from their secret lair," she said. "And if he's close to here, it means their secret lair might just be on that island." Everyone turned to me. "What do you think, Ronald, sounds reasonable, right?"

I stroked my upper lip, where I usually wear a very realistic mustache. "The FIB using this island as their hideout does sound *reasonable*."

"I agree," Jeeves said, "and we should keep sounding reasona—"

"A little *too* reasonable if you ask me."

Jeeves groaned. "Not again."

I let his words slide off me like water off an Australian platypus.

"Remember," I said, "not even my extraordinary parents have been able to find where the FIB is hiding their relics. You heard the man on the radio, the trail is ice cold."

Julianne and Jeeves both looked skeptical, but I finally felt like I had a head of steam.

"Friends, don't you think Francisco and Helen will have already checked the island?" I asked.

"Ronald," Jeeves warned, "you're getting carried away."

"Exactly," I said. "I'm getting carried away from a simple solution and toward something more complicated."

The ship rolled left, and we all slid into Delenda.

"Look," Julianne said with her face smooshed against Jeeves's shoulder. "I know your parents probably have some saying about 'nothing is ever quite what it seems . . .'"

"'Nothing is ever quite what it seems except the sting of the paper wasp,'" I recited. "'Which seems horribly painful and *is* horribly painful.' It's a Francisco Zupan classic."

Another wave sent us sliding back the other direction.

"But maybe things *are* what they seem," Julianne said, as the ship rocked violently. "Maybe the FIB is hiding at Capstone Island."

"I doubt it," I said. "Because I feel myself getting dizzy and my forehead is beading with sweat—two telltale signs of a mystery afoot!"

In this case they were actually telltale signs of Ronald getting seasick. Five seconds later, he flung open the door to the captain's cabin, rushed to the side of the crabbing boat, and threw up into the ocean.

I didn't feel much better. Jeeves, on the other hand, looked perfectly fine. He said he was used to squalls after traveling with Francisco Zupan on a steamer when they were young men. He held the wheel as Delenda settled me in her hammock, then the two of them took turns trading off chess moves and steering the ship. The board had magnets inside to keep the pieces in place, and the table was bolted to the floor.

I don't know how long the storm lasted, because I faded in and out of sleep, trying to keep everything in my stomach right where it was. I just know that at one point I heard Delenda say, "Well, Tom, I believe that's checkmate."

Moments later, Ronald charged back through the door to the cabin. He was soaking wet and his face had a greenish tint, but he also wore that certain Ronald look he gets when he thinks he's figured out something huge.

FACT: And I absolutely had!

10

The Serpent of the Mist!

I burst into the captain's cabin to find Julianne in the hammock and Jeeves and Delenda standing by the wheel.

"I've broken the case wide open!" I announced.

Jeeves turned, looking skeptical. "Before or after you got sick over the rail?"

"*During!*" I said. "I spent a long night on deck with the crew, and they've accepted me as one of their own."

My butler glanced at his watch. "You were on deck for . . . forty minutes."

"And during that time, my new seafaring compatriots told me something that's sure to prove vital in our quest."

Julianne sat up in the hammock.

"We were gazing out at the ocean, as men of the sea often do," I began, leaning against the chess table, "and one of the crabbers said tonight would be just the sort of night that the Serpent of the Mist might appear."

Jeeves's eyebrows arched the second the words left my mouth. "I hesitate to ask, but *what* is—"

"It's a sea monster," I said in a hushed tone. "Giant yellow eyes, spitting smoke, howling with the cries of lost souls."

"The cries of lost souls?" Julianne asked. Her eyebrows were arched too.

FACT: My fellow Danger Gang members are absolute experts in expressive eyebrow movements.

Out ahead of us, I could just barely make out the looming, dark shape of the island. Delenda glanced over her shoulder at me as yet another wave crashed against the bow.

"Who was talking about the Serpent?" she asked.

"The blockheaded one," I said.

"They're mostly all blockheads," the captain replied with a soft little chuckle. "But I think you mean Smollet. He might be the blockhead-iest sailor I've got, always whispering about that serpent."

"Hear that, Ronald?" Julianne said. "The men are superstitious. We need to stay focused on—"

"Hold on now," Delenda interrupted. "I'm not saying that there *isn't* a serpent."

Julianne and Jeeves looked caught off guard, but the sea captain kept piloting the boat, unfazed.

"On stormy nights, especially when the fog is thick, something . . . *appears*," she said.

"What do you mean?" Julianne asked.

Delenda shrugged. "Could be another ship. But it never sends out a radio signal or responds to calls. It's too big to be a fishing boat, and if it were a cruise liner it'd be headed toward Bay City Harbor."

Jeeves gave a wry chuckle. "So your men concluded that it's a fire-breathing sea monster?"

Delenda's expression went ice cold. "Two fishermen went to investigate it last month and never came back. What do you say about that?"

The ship rolled hard to the left.

"Fine," Julianne said, sliding out of her hammock and giving a wary look at the horizon. "So there's something out there, but, Ronald, I still don't see why you think it's important for our case. If Delenda's right about where that man radioed from, and if he's with the rest of the FIB, then we don't need to worry about any sea monsters."

I felt like telling her that the late-night whisperings of superstitious fishermen should never be ignored, or that it's always wise to believe the dazzling theories of Ronald Zupan, or simply that doubting friends are worse than enemies.

Instead I said, "Sato, it's a mystery, and when you're

trying to solve one mystery and other mysteries pop up, you have to wonder if they're all connected, like a maze of clues, leading you—"

"I'm going to stop you right there," Julianne said. "I vote we stay focused on rescuing Josh."

"Seconded!" Jeeves agreed. "Remember, Ronald, this is just a side adventure."

For a moment, it looked like I was outnumbered once again, then Delenda leveled her eyes at me.

"Look for sparks," she said. "That's what everyone talks about when they tell stories of the Serpent—huge explosions of sparks, like it's breathing fire."

I nodded gravely as Delenda eased back on the throttle. Giant rock formations stood out of the water on either side of us, but she navigated past them like a horned owl soaring through a pitch-black forest.

As soon as we were in the protection of Capstone Harbor, the waves were smaller. Finally, the boat stopped rocking. Out ahead, I could just barely make out the craggy shape of the landscape. There were high, jagged cliffs on either side of the port, with a deep valley in between. Everything else was cast in darkness.

Delenda's eyes seemed to slice right through the night. "That your plane?"

She jammed the engine in reverse and wheeled the boat around.

Tied to a piling on a ramshackle dock, our seaplane appeared. Its chrome propeller dipped in the water each time a wave rolled past. A few hundred yards north of the dock, we could make out the shape of a circular building with a domed roof. Clearly it was the old movie theater that Delenda had mentioned.

"Look!" Julianne said.

Lights glowed to life inside. A few seconds later, they snapped off again. I had to admit, it seemed like Delenda had been right about where the FIB took Josh Brigand.

"I can't risk getting any closer to shore," the sea captain said. "One big wave could beach us."

If we were going to investigate the theater, it meant we'd have to dive into the swirling, inky water. Jeeves and I both turned toward Julianne.

After our first adventure, I thought my lifelong fear of the sea was pretty much over. But we were about to swim in a pitch-black bay, with thunder and lightning all around us. Being scared of that isn't a phobia—it's common sense.

Sure, in Borneo we swam through underground tunnels, and almost drowned, but there's something different about the ocean at night. There just is.

"I guess we don't have a choice," Julianne said, swallowing hard.

"If you need help, I'm usually on channel 174 on the radio," Delenda said. "Anything else I can do?"

Jeeves gave her a weak smile. "Keep your ears peeled for the men who captured Josh Brigand."

"Or any talk of the FIB," I added. "Or the Liars' Club, for that matter."

"What are those?" Delenda asked, jamming the engine into reverse to keep from being washed toward shore.

"The Liars' Club is a worldwide villainous network," I said.

Delenda nodded. "And the FIB?"

"They're a local gang that's part of the bigger organization," Julianne said. "Like one very thorny rose on an entire thorny rosebush."

"I'll scan the radio," the captain replied.

I thought to ask her to keep a lookout for the Serpent of the Mist, too, but talk of sea monsters could wait. Julianne already seemed nervous enough about swimming in the bay.

We thanked Delenda and started toward the door. As Jeeves turned the handle, she called to him. "Hey, Tom. It's polite for me, the winner of our chess game, to offer you, the loser, a rematch."

Jeeves's thin lips curved into a slight smile. "I'd enjoy that," he said, stepping back into the driving rain. "That is, if we make it out of this alive."

11

Terrible Yellow Eyes!

I jumped over the rail of the ship first. The cold water sent a rush of chills through my body. A second later, Julianne and Jeeves sputtered to the surface beside me and we swam for the rotting dock.

Delenda angled the boat, so that its light shone on the water. Now we could see the flat, slick pieces of seaweed writhing like ribbon eels on the surface of the ocean.

FACT: Thinking about ribbon eels is an excellent way to make a tired adventurer swim faster.

By the time the crabbing boat left the harbor, we'd dragged ourselves up onto the dock. We were shivering and soaked to the bone. Julianne's shoes squelched with water, and I could hear her teeth chattering.

We started down the dock and after about twenty steps, came to the Zupan seaplane. I stopped and peered through the window. It was empty. I jiggled the handle. Locked.

"The scalawags locked us out of our own plane!" I yelled to my friends over the storm.

I tugged at the handle again, harder this time. When it didn't budge, I set a foot against the plane's body and jerked it with all my might.

"Wait," Julianne said, "if we think the FIB is in the theater, why bother with the plane?"

I peered in the window. "Every plane in my parents' fleet has been outfitted by the manager of Zupan Hangar, Elexander Davidson. My parents once survived for three months in the Albanian highlands with one of his supply cases."

"I forgot about that," Jeeves said, snapping his fingers. "You're absolutely right!"

I noticed that Julianne had turned back toward the ocean, and I stopped tugging at the door to follow her sightline.

"Something wrong, Sato?"

She raised a hand to point into the endless darkness. "Do you see a boat?"

I took a few steps forward and squinted into the distance. "You mean the one we just got off? The one full of clumsy crabbers?"

"No," Julianne said. "Way out there."

Ronald Zupan has the eyesight of a white-bellied sea eagle . . . and I couldn't see a thing.

"Strange," she muttered after a long minute. "Probably nothing."

"Sato, nothing is ever nothing," I argued. "As my mother says, 'Always question the shapes you see out at sea.' Maybe it was the Serpent of the—"

"It was just a boat, Ronald. Small . . . the kind that could fit only one person."

I looked again. Whatever it was, it seemed to trouble my adventure partner.

"Aha!" Jeeves said.

Julianne and I both turned around. The door of the plane was open and the butler was beaming. He held up a thin piece of leather.

"I picked the lock with my shoelace," he said, leaning over the pilot's seat to rummage for Elexander's supply kit. "Your father taught me how to do it ages ago, back in Zanzibar."

It'd been a few hours since I'd thought of my parents. We needed to radio them. I just wanted to have a few good leads first, so they'd know that their brave son had this side adventure under control.

I noticed that Julianne was staring off into the distance again, but this time I could see right away what she was looking at. The light of a single, flickering lantern bounced around inside the old theater.

"Someone's still there," she said as Jeeves dragged a wooden crate out of the plane and wrestled it down onto the dock.

"Where?" the good butler asked between heavy breaths. We pointed to the lantern light.

"I suppose that's where we begin," he said. "Hopefully Davidson packed a few swords. Or maybe a cricket bat."

I knelt down and pried open the crate. It was held together with skinny nails and came apart easily. There was straw inside, covering whatever adventure supplies Elexander had stored away.

"Here's a blanket," I called to my friends. "And . . . four tins of anchovies. And . . ."

I dug my hand back into the crate and found a bottle of champagne, some cheese and crackers, a leather satchel, matches, and a box of sparklers. I dug deeper, sure that at any second I'd touch the cold steel of a sword, but came up empty handed.

"No weapons?" I asked, holding up a fistful of straw.

Jeeves looked down at our shabby supplies. "Crackers, cheese, champagne, sparklers, and a blanket—with a satchel to carry them all. I think Elexander expected whoever was flying the seaplane to have a picnic."

"You forgot to mention the anchovies," I said. "Maybe we'll meet a scoundrel who's allergic to canned fish."

Even though they seemed useless, we loaded the things into the leather satchel. As the great Francisco Zupan says, "'Supplies are important to any adventure . . . particularly insect repellent.'"

Not that we had any insect repellent.

The storm had let up a little and the rain was more of a drizzle. We could see the fuzzy glow of the half-moon above us, still blocked by clouds. The theater was farther off than it had looked, and the path was dark.

Ronald led the way, with Jeeves behind him. I trailed behind and couldn't stop myself from turning around every few feet. First there had been that strange car that drove after our taxi. Then, when we climbed onto the dock, I swore I saw a boat on the crest of a wave.

> I was starting to get a strange feeling that someone was following us, but decided that the only thing to do was keep moving.

"*Stop!*" I called.

There was rustling behind a tree and it froze me in my tracks. My heart hammered like the heart of a master adventurer who is not at all afraid but simply ready to face danger head-on.

"Sato!" I said, waving her toward me. "There's something back there!"

My friends crowded close. Something was sniffing and scratching on the other side of a palm tree. Perhaps it was an FIB scoundrel, waiting to ambush us.

I reached into the satchel and grabbed the cheese wedge. It wasn't much, but my parents once fought a gang of smugglers in Bangladesh with two Belgian waffles and a cantaloupe. I passed the champagne bottle to Jeeves and two tins of anchovies to Julianne.

"Come out, you rogues!" I boomed. "The Danger Gang is here."

"Hand over Josh Brigand," Julianne added. "We've got . . . weapons."

No sooner had she said it than three sets of terrible yellow eyes appeared out of the gloom, glaring right at us.

12

Blackout!

I took a step closer and squinted into the darkness. The yellow eyes belonged to some sort of small animal. From my best guess, they were a miniature species of coyote or maybe baby jackals.

The only difference was that the odd creatures had giant, pointy ears.

"Sato," I said, "do you recognize these strange specimens?"

"I don't think so," she answered.

The animals yapped and nipped at one another, diving and rolling on the grass.

"They don't *seem* dangerous," Jeeves said. "They're almost . . . sort of *cute*, aren't they?"

"Nothing like the clouded leopard we faced in Borneo,"

Julianne said. "It would take a whole pack of these to do us any . . ."

She trailed off as two more of the feral beasts capered into a clearing. A second later, we heard rustling, spun around, and saw another four sets of eyes. Whatever the animals were, they were inching closer—only to dive out of sight every time we made the slightest move.

We kept walking down the abandoned lane, steps quickening. The strange creatures trotted alongside us—doubling, then tripling in number. It was enough to make a master adventurer forget about Josh Brigand or the FIB.

As we drew closer to the theater, still more of the odd animals popped out of the bushes. Soon, we had at least fifty of them tracking our every move. They were getting bolder too, prowling closer.

"I have an idea," Julianne said.

She peeled open one of the tins of anchovies, grabbed an oily fistful, and threw them as far as she could. The whole sea of pointy ears turned away from us at once and dashed for the fish.

I grinned at my adventure partner. "Sato, that—"

"Wasn't your best idea, I'm afraid," Jeeves interrupted.

The animals were already racing back to us, and there were twice as many now. When Julianne didn't give them anything else, they let out little dissatisfied sniffs and snarls.

"The theater is only twenty steps away," Jeeves said. "We could—"

"Go!" Julianne threw the entire tin, and we sprinted for the door.

We hadn't gone five feet before the beasts were on our heels again, yipping in a chorus. Our drenched shoes slapped across the pavement and hundreds of tiny feet padded along after us.

I skidded to the door first. There was a hole where the deadbolt should have been. My toe kicked something, and I saw the lock. Some scalawag had chiseled it out of the wooden frame.

Seeing the smashed lock reminded me that we might be walking right into an FIB trap set up by Dirk Grimple or his boss. We'd been so worried about the rabid animals behind us that we'd completely forgotten about the deadly villains that might be ahead.

"Friends," I said, "as we enter, I'm reminded of the words of Francisco—"

"Ronald," Julianne interrupted, pushing me forward, "talk inside."

I glanced over my shoulder. The moon had broken through the clouds completely now, and I could see the animals more clearly. They were like small dogs with pinched faces and those strange, oversized ears. They weren't scared of us anymore, either. Instead, they were inching closer as one massive group.

"Where could they be coming from?" Jeeves cried.

I shoved the door. There was something blocking it, but it

didn't push against me the way a fearsome enemy would have. Julianne peeled open another tin of anchovies and hurled it as far as she could. I used all my Zupanian might to force the door open and then slipped through a thin gap.

"This way!" I said.

My friends squeezed in after me just as the beasts came charging back. We slammed the door shut and Julianne held it closed. A couch had been shoved up against it, and Jeeves and I pushed it back into place. The strange animals were left whining and clawing hopelessly against the wood.

We found ourselves in a cavernous lobby, cast in darkness.

"Friends," I said, "these FIB goons have us at a severe disadvantage. We have no weapons, no light, and no idea where they took their captive."

"I don't like those odds," Julianne said.

"Me neither," Jeeves agreed. "Ah, but here's one problem solved."

He flipped a switch and ten lamps hummed to life around the lobby. There was an empty concession stand to our right and two sweeping staircases leading to the balcony on either side of the room. Opposite us, there were engraved swinging doors. I deduced that they probably opened into the theater.

"Now what?" Julianne asked.

It was a fair question. Anchovies might have held the pack

of animals at bay, but they wouldn't defeat the FIB. We needed a way to defend ourselves.

The three of us gazed silently around the room. There wasn't much that could be useful. An old popcorn maker, but that was too heavy; a few tattered movie posters, but those were too light.

Julianne ran over to a giant espresso machine sitting in an alcove underneath one of the staircases.

"Tired, Sato?" I asked my adventure partner. "Helen Zupan often says, 'If you're feeling like you need a week of sleep, even a weak cup of coffee can—'"

Crack! Julianne snapped one arm off the machine and weighed it in her hands. It was oddly shaped, but no rogue would be eager to be clubbed by it. Jeeves followed her lead—wrenching the oval lid off the contraption and giving it a few practice swings. That left me with a chrome coffee canister. I held it over my head, ready to throw it at any enemy I spotted.

Thunk! We heard a sound echo in the theater. Someone was still there.

"I *knew* we should have brought a cobra," I whispered.

Julianne dimmed the lights until they cast just enough glow for us to see one another. We slipped through the doors to the theater and started walking down the center aisle, toward the screen. I bent low to inspect the carpet.

"What are you looking for?" Jeeves whispered.

"Clues," I said. "Signs of villainy afoot."

"Speaking of 'a foot' . . ." Julianne held up a single white-and-tan saddle shoe.

It was Brigand's all right. I'd noticed them back in Bay City. The man may not be as adventurous as Ronald Zupan, but he *does* have style.

"Maybe Josh kicked off the other one somewhere," Julianne said. "Like leaving breadcrumbs."

She and Jeeves fanned out to opposite sides of the theater. I flipped to a familiar page in my adventure journal.

"Sometimes the best clues aren't objects," I read aloud, "they're seen or heard or smelled."

"I only smell dust and stale popcorn," Julianne said, off to my left.

I hopped up onto the stage, still holding the coffee canister, and slipped between the thick velvet curtains.

"Sometimes it's as simple as a change of breeze," I said, "like when my parents were lost in the Egyptian desert. That time they actually *felt* a clue."

FACT: At that moment something came soaring toward me and I felt a clue of my own: a sandbag, smashing me right behind the ear.

My vision exploded with a rush of stars and color. Then my legs turned into Burmese rubber and everything went black.

Ronald groaned, and his coffee canister
clanged to the ground.

"What happened?" Jeeves yelled, sprinting
for the stage.

"I have another sandbag!" a voice
warned. It was a young boy, by the sound
of it. "Don't come up here!"

The voice came from overhead, in the
catwalks. "Are you . . . are you good guys
or . . . bad guys?"

Jeeves stopped moving and stared at me.

"Good guys," I said.

"That's what bad guys would say," the boy replied.

"Have you heard of the famous Zupan family?" Jeeves asked.

"No," the boy said.

I pulled myself up onto the stage. "The people who came into this theater earlier tonight, they were bad guys, right? Except their captive."

"Don't come any closer," the boy said.

I put my hand on the velvet curtain. "Well, those men are our enemies. If they're bad guys, then we—"

"You could still be bad." The voice was trembling. "Bad guys can chase other bad guys."

I hesitated, then pushed the curtain aside. "We need to see if our friend is okay. He needs our help."

"Don't—"

"It's our duty," Jeeves interrupted. He hopped onto the stage and we both stepped past the velvet curtain.

There was a long pause before the voice

spoke again. "Well . . . that doesn't seem like something bad guys would say."

Seconds later, dozens of lamps all around the theater hummed to life.

13

Hardheaded!

We found Ronald just on the other side of the curtain, sprawled on the ground. He had a bump swelling up behind his left ear, but his breathing was steady. A sandbag tied to a rope sat next to him.

"He'll be okay, right?" I asked.

"He's got the thickest skull of any person I've ever met," Jeeves replied. "He'll be fine."

We heard movement a few feet away and glanced up. The boy had slipped quietly down from an iron ladder and was watching us from across the stage. He had thick, curly black hair, dark skin, and hazel eyes. My best guess put him at eight years old.

"I thought he was going to find me,"
he said. "That's why I dropped the
sandbag."

Jeeves touched the back of his hand to
Ronald's cheek. "We swam in the bay and
he's got a chill. Do you know any place
where we might warm up?"

The boy hesitated for a second, then
nodded. "My mom and I have an apartment
upstairs. There's a fireplace."

Jeeves hoisted Ronald over his shoulder,
and the boy led us into the lobby and
up one of the sweeping staircases. There
was a cozy apartment with two desks
and a little kitchenette. The room had one
glass window looking out over the theater,
with a film projector pointing at the
screen.

There were embers still glowing in the
fireplace. Jeeves peeled off Ronald's wet
shirt and rolled him up in a blanket on the
carpet. We leaned over him together and
listened to his breathing.

"Do people usually stay knocked out this
long?" I asked.

Jeeves lifted one shoulder. "Not sure.
If he doesn't wake up in . . ." He checked

his watch. "Ten minutes, then we'll have to get him back to Bay City."

For the first time I realized that I was shivering too. The boy noticed and ducked into a second room. He came back with a whole armful of blankets and towels. He also gave me a thick wool sweater.

"My name is Elias," he said. "I live here with my mom." He clicked on a hot plate and filled a small pot with cocoa powder and milk. "She's a scientist, here on a project. We just started a few weeks ago."

It was raining again, and we could hear it pinging on the domed roof of the theater. Jeeves and I dragged chairs next to the fire while Elias finished the cocoa.

"What's your mother studying?" Jeeves asked.

"You didn't happen to see any animals outside, did you?"

"Six hundred or so," I said. "Maybe more."

Elias gave me a little smirk and passed me a cup of cocoa. "Those are fennec foxes. They come from Algeria, just like my mom."

"What are foxes from Algeria doing on
Capstone Island?" Jeeves asked.

Elias took a long sip of his cocoa and
sat down in a third seat. I could tell he
was starting to feel safe. His eyes twinkled
a little in the firelight. "Have you ever
heard of an actor named Josh Brigand?"

Jeeves shot me a glance.

I leaned forward in my seat. "Believe it
or not, Josh Brigand is the reason we're
here."

"Us too!" Elias said. He pointed to the

wall, which was hung with black-and-white photos. I could see that each one was for a different Capstone movie—*Hail, Rome!*, *The Sinking of the Titanic*, *The Search for the Sundance Kid*, *The Sinking of the Titanic II*.

"A few years ago, Josh Brigand shot a movie here for Capstone Pictures," Elias went on. "In it, his plane crashed and he had to wander the rocky desert for days without water."

"My grandfather and I saw that one," I said. "It's called *Stranded in an Ancient Land*."

"Well," Elias said, "when they were filming, the movie crew brought in a dozen fennec foxes, so that it would look more like the Sahara Desert. But when the movie wrapped, they left the animals behind."

"So they've completely overrun the island?" Jeeves asked.

Elias took a sip of cocoa and nodded. "The foxes keep having babies because there are no predators. So my mom got an offer from the Capstone Island Science Trust to study them for a year." He stopped short, looked at Jeeves and me, and then spoke again, in a low voice. "But strange things have been happening ever since we arrived."

"What sorts of things?" I asked.

"People come onto the island late at night. Boats tie up or drift in the harbor. Sometimes they light bonfires on the beaches. Then tonight, a group of men broke into the theater when I was asleep."

"Where's your mom?"

"The foxes are more active after dark," Elias said. "So every night she has to go watch them. A few times she took me, but then I was groggy the whole next day."

Jeeves and I waited for him to go on. I could see that there was something else.

"Also, Mom said not to talk about it, because it's not scientifically possible, but . . . a few nights ago, there was something in the fog . . . offshore. It looked . . . it looked—"

"Like it had glowing eyes and was spitting fire?" I asked.

FACT: Ronald Zupan had been awake for at least three minutes, just waiting for the perfect moment to join the conversation!

I leaped to my feet, then staggered again. The blankets were tangled around my ankles and my head throbbed. Also, I didn't have a shirt on.

"Ronald," Jeeves said, "meet Elias."

I wrapped one of the blankets around my shoulders like an Argentinian serape and stared down at the young stranger.

"Sorry about your head," Elias said.

"Ronald Zupan is highly resistant to pain," I replied.

"You are? That's cool!" His face shifted a little. "I would've been hurt."

I reached behind my ear and traced my wound, wincing. "What were you saying about something in the fog?"

Elias wet his lips but Jeeves held up a hand to stop him. "Sorry, but we don't have time for more Serpent of the Mist talk just now."

"Jeeves," I said, "don't you see that the Serpent might be—"

"*Side adventure*," the butler sang. "And I believe in a side adventure, the only rule is: keep things simple." He looked to Elias. "Now, which way did you say the kidnappers went?"

"There's a ladder behind the curtain. It leads to the boiler room. They went in there."

In seconds, we were racing down the sweeping staircase, into the lobby of the theater and toward the spot where I was knocked out.

We ducked past the velvet curtain and Elias pointed to an open hatch, with a ladder disappearing into the darkness.

"I was in the catwalk, trying to decide what to do when you all rushed in. I thought you were more bad guys, so . . ."

My eyes darted over to the sandbag that had floored me.

"Are we following them?" Julianne asked.

Elias slipped away for a second and came back with a lantern. "My mom set these around the theater because the storms sometimes knock the power out."

He handed it to Julianne with a book of matches. She lit the wick and turned the knob so that it was barely burning.

"The caretaker of the island told me not to explore down there," Elias said. "She read me a poem about how it's cursed . . ." He grinned. "But I did it anyway."

"What did you find?" Jeeves asked.

"Tunnels," Elias said. "There are old tunnels leading all directions."

I peered down into the boiler room but couldn't see much. "Abandoned mine shafts? Ancient catacombs?"

Elias shook his head. "There was a book left behind when my mom and I got here. It's called *The Capstone Moving Picture Company: The First 30 Years.* There's a part where it says that when the company bought the island they dug a bunch of tunnels, so that the surface could look deserted in the movies. The only two buildings are this one and the caretaker's house."

"Did the book say what's down there?" Julianne asked.

"It's supposed to be everything they'd need for a production—dressing rooms, prop closets, a dining hall . . ."

Jeeves bulged his lower lip with his tongue. "The FIB might have moved in when the movie company left."

I started down the ladder. "There's only one way to find out."

"Without swords?" Jeeves asked. "Are we going to protect ourselves with a cheese wedge and a bottle of champagne?"

I gave him a winning smile. "Think of how impressed my parents would be by *that*."

Jeeves groaned. "And what happens when—"

"*If* we see something," I interrupted, "we'll double back here and come up with a plan. It's a scouting mission. Like Francisco and Helen in the Temple of Tikal."

Jeeves turned to Julianne.

She shrugged. "It's really our only choice. Besides, we have the pieces of the coffee machine."

"Excellent," Jeeves said. "Maybe we can offer them all espressos right before they pummel us."

Just as I climbed onto the ladder, Elias touched my shoulder.

"I'm not coming. When my mom gets back, she'll see the broken lock. I don't want to scare her."

I nodded. "You can still help us. Just

stay close. We might have to retreat back to the theater."

"I'll get a few more sandbags ready," Elias said.

A thought struck me. "One more thing. Do you think I could borrow that book, the one about the island? It might have something we need to know."

"Sure thing!"

As Elias sprinted up the theater aisle, I lowered myself down the ladder—every rung bringing me closer to a meeting with the FIB.

14

The Edge of Danger!

As soon as Elias dropped the book down to Julianne, she tucked it inside our satchel.

"Good luck!" Elias called.

The light in the theater silhouetted him.

"The Danger Gang doesn't need luck!" I said. "And we never forget a friend!"

"The Danger Gang," Elias repeated. "That sounds cool. How could I become a member?"

I looked at my partner in dazzling schemes. She turned up her palms and shrugged.

"Well . . . we haven't discussed how someone would join," I said. "What would you say to starting out as a 'temporary member' and—"

"*Deal!*" Elias said. "You can count on me, temporary member of the Danger Gang."

I thanked him and stepped away from the trapdoor. Julianne lengthened the wick on our lantern.

"The dastardly dogs clearly knew about the tunnels when they broke into the theater," I said. "They're either using them to get somewhere without being discovered, or—"

"Or *this* is the somewhere they're trying to get to," Jeeves finished. "It's secret and has multiple entry points—a perfect hideout."

"Well," Julianne said with the lantern in one hand and the arm of the coffee maker in the other, "we're about to find out."

We stood by the boiler for a long minute, with steam coming off our wet clothes. Finally, I stepped forward and threw open the room's only door. Sure enough, we were in a tunnel—dark and silent.

We crept along, with the lantern casting its light a few feet ahead of us. It was as quiet as a hibernating wood frog, and there was a certain heavy stillness in the air. You could just *feel* that you were deep below the earth.

We moved through the tunnels in complete silence. The floors were made of cold, polished concrete, and our wet shoes squished with each step. Every twenty feet there was a door. Some were closed and others stood half-open, but we didn't slow down enough to look inside.

"It's almost like walking through the halls of Silver Hills Middle School on the first day of summer," Julianne muttered.

"Sato," I said, "we have more than enough to worry about without bringing up public school."

"It's not *that* bad," Julianne said. "Jeez."

We walked a half mile or so without seeing anything. Finally, the tunnel curved slightly and we stopped—ready for whatever might leap out at us. But it wasn't goons that we saw next; it was a crossroads. The tunnel branched off in three directions.

I knelt at the entrance to each path, peering close to the ground to look for disturbances in the dust. After a minute, I turned to my friends and shrugged.

"Just like old Jeff Brimley not to leave a clue," I said. "A piece of fabric, or another shoe or—"

I was interrupted by the distant echoes of Brigand's voice bouncing down one of the tunnels.

"*Help!*" the movie star begged. "*Helllllp!*"

"That good enough?" Julianne asked, charging after the voice.

Jeeves and I followed her as fast as we could. Soon the doors we passed started to blur, and the only sounds we could hear were the jangling of the lantern, the squelching of our shoes on the concrete, and our own heavy breathing.

We ran without coming to any more splits for a long time. Finally, we saw a sharp turn ahead and skidded to a halt. We peered around the corner. There was a rectangle of dark blue amid all the blackness.

"Slowly," Jeeves said, raising the lid of the coffee maker. "*Slowly.*"

We crept forward, ears perked for any sound. After twenty steps, we could see that the blue rectangle was an open door, which emptied onto a moonlit meadow. It looked like the storm had broken completely.

Julianne put down the lantern and we stepped outside with our pieces of coffee maker held high. There were no signs of the FIB or Josh Brigand. There didn't seem to be anyone at all.

Jeeves walked forward fifty feet, then reared back as if he'd been stung by a scorpion.

"What is it?" I called.

"Come here," he said. *"But be careful."*

Julianne and I crept forward. Jeeves was crouching with his arms wide, as if to hold us back, still gripping the lid to the coffee machine in one hand.

"I *hate* heights," he whispered, voice trembling.

We drew up alongside him. Julianne let out a little whistle.

> **FACT: We'd come to the edge of a cliff—two hundred feet tall if it was an inch.**

I pointed to the beam of a flashlight, far below us. "That must be them."

A second later the light started to move, then we heard a dull buzz.

"They're in a boat!" Julianne said. "We have to do something!"

I looked down at the cold water. "We could—"

"If we jumped we would die," Jeeves said. "From fifty feet, fine. Maybe seventy-five in a pinch."

"We jumped off a cliff in Borneo that was a hundred," I said.

Jeeves scoffed. "Not a memory I'm fond of, but this is double that. From this high, the water would feel like a slab of stone."

Jeeves seemed to know *way* too much about jumping from cliffs. I guess when you're the butler for a family like the Zupans, you learn those sorts of things. Anyway, I have to admit I was only half listening.

Why had the FIB come to Capstone Island if they were only going to disappear again? How had they known about the tunnels? Most of all, where were they going now?

I wanted to write some notes in my adventure journal, so I ran to grab the lantern. Back at the cliff, I wrote down

everything that had been said over the
radio—hoping desperately to find a clue.

"There's a way down!" I called to my partner in dazzling schemes.

Jeeves and I had been disagreeing about how the kidnappers got to their boat when he practically kicked the top rung of an iron ladder.

"See that?" I said, patting him on the back. "Once again, our teamwork leads to a discovery."

Julianne trotted toward us. It wasn't actually one ladder; it was at least ten, built in sections. Every thirty feet there was a platform, like a giant fire escape bolted to the side of the cliff. The storm clouds had cleared, but it was still too dark to see what was at the very bottom.

"Where might they be racing off to?" Jeeves asked, with the wind tossing his wispy hair.

Julianne and I shook our heads. We needed a crucial clue or a dazzling deduction. I'd have settled for a half-baked hunch. Instead, we saw a flashing blue light, bouncing and bobbing behind us.

We wheeled around just as a Jeep rumbled into view, skidding to a halt between the tunnel door and our spot on the cliff. A rough voice crackled over the intercom.

"This is the Capstone Island Security Team. Stay where you are."

15

The Brothers Grin!

I looked over my shoulder and saw that the light at the bow of the FIB boat was just the tiniest dot now. The villains were getting away.

I turned back toward the Jeep. Dawn was only a few hours off and it was getting easier to see. Two tough-looking men sprang from the car. They were both shorter than Jeeves but twice as thick, with arms that stretched their blue uniforms.

One man wore a mustache, but not the type favored by master adventurers like Ronald Zupan. It was the type favored by Siberian walruses, with bristles that completely covered his upper lip.

The other man wore a navy-blue sailor's hat with a gold anchor on it. His eyes were watery, and he held a toothpick pressed between his thin lips.

"Who are you three?" the man with the mustache

demanded, looking us up and down. "And what are you doing on Capstone Island?"

I straightened up. "We're the founding members of the—"

"Kids Cozy Camping Club," Julianne interrupted, shooting me a look.

The man with the sailor's hat flicked his toothpick to the ground. "Well, you're not supposed to camp here without permission from the caretaker." He glanced sideways at his partner. "How do you think this all sounds, Bill?"

The officer called Bill threw the door to the tunnel shut. It closed with a heavy *CLANG!*

"Looks to me like they were in the tunnels, Jake," Bill said. "And *no one* is supposed to be in the tunnels."

He unbuttoned a wooden nightstick off his belt and twirled it a few times. "Get in the Jeep."

I eyed Jeeves and Julianne. It didn't look good for us, but we'd been in tighter spots. We were close to a sheer cliff, facing two brawny men with nightsticks, and our only weapons were pieces of an antique coffee maker and some picnic supplies.

Still, we could fight. Or we could pretend like we were going with them, then run. Or we could even—

"Whatever you say!" Julianne said in a cheery voice. She trotted over to the Jeep, stepped up on a tire, and slid into the back seat.

Here's the thing: the kidnappers were cruising away with Josh Brigand. What were we going to do next? Chase them without a boat? Cross the island with all the foxes?

The trail was cold. So when two men drive up, saying they're security for an abandoned island, you think, *This smells fishy,* and *If I play my cards right, I just might learn something.*

Jeeves gave me a baffled shrug. "I suppose it's the best option we've got."

He approached the Jeep and folded his long legs into the back seat. I heard a little squeak off to my right, and I saw the shadowy outline of a fennec fox watching me. Then another popped up beside it.

"They found us!" Bill yelled. "Start the motor!"

He ran to the car and dove into the passenger side. Jake was already in the driver's seat. He leaned out the window and slapped the door. "It's come with us or stay with the foxes, kid."

Thirty foxes prowled close, their yellow eyes focused just on me. They snarled and pawed the ground.

"Maybe this isn't a bad idea after all," I said.

I ran and slid into the car next to Jeeves. We bucked along a rocky path, up another hill, and down into the valley below. The eyes of foxes shone out of the darkness in every direction, but they kept their distance.

"We have to get you two warmed up," Jeeves said. "I wish these pieces of the coffee machine could actually brew something hot."

"Master adventurers never get cold," I insisted. "I'm perfectly fine."

"That might be more believable if your teeth weren't chattering," Jeeves said, watching the rocky track.

There was a glass partition between the front seat and back seat of the Jeep. Taped onto the glass were pictures of each man with their names printed below.

"'Security Officers Jake and Bill Grin,'" Julianne read aloud.

"We're brothers," Bill grunted.

My partner in dazzling schemes gave a crooked smile. "You don't say?"

"You're the Brothers Grin," Jeeves said. "Like the Brothers Grimm."

Bill jerked around to face him. "The name is *Grin* not Grimm."

"Grin," Jake repeated. "With an 'N.'"

"Yes, yes," Jeeves said, "but it *sounds* like Grimm, doesn't it? Plus your names are Bill and Jake and theirs were Wilhelm and Jacob. Your parents must have—"

"*Do we tease you about your name?*" Bill boomed, his mustache quivering.

"*No!*" Jake shouted. "*We* tried *to bring you along peacefully!*"

"I just meant—"

"*Our parents liked fairy tales, okay?*" Jake screamed.

"No, I—"

Julianne patted Jeeves's knee. "Just let this one go."

"I wasn't teasing," Jeeves muttered. "I was simply curious. I mean . . ."

Bill's mustache started twitching again and Jeeves trailed off. Jake pulled the wheel to the right as the Jeep bounced over a fallen yucca tree.

After a few minutes, Bill wheeled around suddenly. "It's Grin, with an 'N.' Understand?"

"Quite," Jeeves whispered.

Jake Grin steered the car across the rocky landscape. Soon, the headlights shone on a windswept house, tucked beneath a tall rock outcropping.

"That's where the caretaker lives," Bill said, pointing at it. "And you better be careful, because she'll make you *grim* if you lie to her."

16

No Place Like Hode!

We approached a house surrounded by a chicken wire fence and rattled to a halt in front of a wooden gate.

Jake motioned to his brother. "Go ahead. I'm driving."

Bill stayed in his seat.

"Stop it," Jake said. "You know the foxes don't like the sound of motors!"

Bill reached a hand up and touched his left earlobe. I leaned forward and saw that its bottom half was missing.

"That happened a year ago," Jake said. "Who needs an earlobe anyway?"

"*I* liked *that earlobe!*" Bill boomed.

The two of them glared at each other. Neither blinked. If the Danger Gang had been trying to plot a dazzling escape, it would have made the perfect distraction.

Actually, it *did* make the perfect distraction—
I'd hopped out of the car and opened the
gate before the Brothers Grin even noticed.
As I swung it wide, I saw that the sky
had already started to turn purple. Then,
about a quarter mile away, I saw
something else.

I mean someone else. Someone in a
cape, ducking low and running over the crest
of a hill.

Who wears capes? I thought. More
than that, who runs across hills in capes—
dodging fennec foxes and leaping off rocks?

I had the answer, of course. It
was the same kind of person who follows
taxicabs with their headlights off. The
same type who sails a small craft through
a raging storm.

If I were Ronald, now would be a
good time to say, "FACT: We were
definitely being followed."

The Brothers Grin were still staring each other down,
breathing in short angry bursts. They didn't even notice that
Julianne wasn't in the car until Jeeves told them.

"Everything okay?" I asked my adventure partner as

soon as Jake had parked. "You look like you've seen a ghost."

She just stared blankly ahead, like a dazed koala.

Jake flicked another chewed-up toothpick on the ground and started toward the door. His brother followed him, combing his bristly hair with his fingers.

I fell back to whisper to my compatriots. "When Francisco and Helen enter the home of a mysterious stranger, they use a secret phrase. Something either of them can slip into conversation to let the other person know 'we need to leave.'"

"Good," Jeeves said softly. "What should ours be?"

"Grappling hooks," I suggested.

"How will you work grappling hooks into conversation?" Jeeves asked. "How about 'cucumber sandwiches'?"

"We should use fake names," Julianne said under her breath.

I frowned. "Sato, I think 'fake names' is a little odd for a safety phrase."

"No, I meant—"

The Brothers Grin wheeled around and shushed us. Bill rapped three times on the door, and they both edged backward, waving us onto the porch.

The sky had turned purple, so we could see some of the details of the house. It was built like most of the houses in Bay City. There were flower boxes on the windowsills and pale blue shutters on the windows.

I looked up and saw a little curl of smoke trailing out of the chimney. My shoes brushed against the bristles of a doormat.

I muttered the words written on it. "'There's no place like—'"

"Hode," came a sweet, purring voice.

A woman had soundlessly opened the door. Her eyes were pale blue and watery. She had long silver hair that rippled across her shoulders, like one shimmering sheet.

"I bought twenty of these misspelled doormats for two dollars." She leaned forward like telling a secret. "Then I named those cliffs Hode Point and my home the Hode House. I have enough of them to last me forever."

"Unless you move," Jeeves quipped.

The woman's jaw set. "Oh, I could never leave Hode House. *Never.*"

Julianne reached out a hand. "I'm . . . Madeline Hammersmith."

"Ah yes," Jeeves said, "and I'm . . . Abernathy Jones."

I quickly deduced that "fake names" hadn't been Julianne's idea for a safety phrase; she was telling us to *give* fake names.

FACT: It had been a long night, and the Zupanian brain was in no condition to come up with an alias.

I stalled by kneeling down to tie my shoe. "My name is . . . *Feet . . . eee . . . Hode . . . mat.*"

"Feety Hodematt?" the woman asked. "Is that Dutch?"

"Indeed," I said, standing to shake her thin hand. "Dutch. Quite Dutch."

The woman rolled her shoulders back. "My name is Vivienne DuVoe. I'm the poetess-in-residence and chief caretaker of this island." She waved us inside. "Come now, you three look like you're freezing."

The woman wore a silk dressing robe over faded jeans and a baggy knit sweater. She pulled the robe tight around her thin frame.

"Wipe your feet," she said, "and leave those pieces of coffee maker. I already prepared tea."

17

Strange Brew!

We hesitated, then wiped our feet on the misspelled door-mat. I set my coffee canister by the coat rack and Jeeves did the same with his lid, but from the corner of my eye, I saw Julianne slip the arm of the espresso filter up the sleeve of her sweater.

The Brothers Grin seemed to think this was the signal to clomp up onto the porch behind us, but Vivienne DuVoe blocked them. She pressed a piece of paper to Bill's chest like she was pinning it to a corkboard.

"Send this telegram," she said. "Then come back here straightaway. Ten minutes."

Bill's mustache twitched again, but he didn't argue. He just shuffled back a little, with Jake beside him. Vivienne swung the door shut in their faces.

The inside of the house was still and cozy. Our hostess led us into a sitting room. The cabinets were all lined with crystal figurines. There were Russian nesting dolls, unpacked and standing in orderly rows. A bed of coals glowed in the fireplace.

In the center of the room there was a table set with a steaming kettle of tea, three porcelain teacups, and a plate of butter cookies.

"Please, have some tea," Vivienne said, "I just brewed it."

Jeeves poured himself a cup immediately and took a long sip. "I've needed a spot of tea for quite some time. Thank you."

Vivienne's eyes glittered as she watched him. Then she turned to us. "What about you two? Madeline? Feety? Tea is such a peaceful way to start the morning, don't you think?"

She poured two more cups and handed them to Julianne and me. I glanced at the table but didn't see any sugar.

"Drink up," Vivienne chirped with a smile.

FACT: Ronald Zupan will suffer a night filled with cold water, dark tunnels, and strange scalawags, but he won't tolerate bitter tea.

I lifted the cup but kept my lips pressed tight, not swallowing a drop. Julianne took a few sips, then frowned, studying the tea set. "You're not having any?"

Vivienne waved a hand. "I rose early. I find mornings on this island to be so very peaceful."

"Not *our* morning," Julianne said, taking another slow sip. "Did you send the Brothers Grin to pick us up?"

"You *were* trespassing," Vivienne said with a syrupy smile.

Julianne studied our hostess over the rim of her teacup. "The Grins remind me of two characters in Josh Brigand's detective movie," she said. "*The Longest Midnight.*"

I said that because I hoped she might react to hearing Josh's name. I was looking for something small—a mouth twitch, an arched eyebrow, a clenched jaw . . . anything to show that she knew him.

Our hostess smoothed the tablecloth with one hand and offered a thin smile. "I don't watch that nonsense. I'm a writer of sophistication."

"What do you write?" I asked.

"Poems about the wind and the cliffs and the ocean," Vivienne replied. She said "poems" as if it were actually two words—*poe-emms*—and both words had been dipped in honey. "The owner of this island has given me this cabin, where I can breathe the briny salt air, alone with my journal."

She patted the pocket of her dressing gown. I could see a thin blue notebook peeking out.

Vivienne DuVoe kept staring dreamily at the mint-colored wallpaper. Her smile felt as fake as the mustache Ronald likes to wear.

"Vivienne, I envy this privacy," Jeeves said in a sleepy voice. "No one cutting open your toothpaste tube to search for the Lost Jewel of Marrakesh."

I shot him a look. "I only did that once."

"Once was more than enough, *Feety*," he said, slurring his words.

Vivienne leaned over from her chair to pour him more tea. "Is that why you've come to Capstone Island? For solitude, or . . . for some other reason?"

This woman knew something, and I wanted her to keep talking. I didn't think it was smart to tell her why we were there, though. In my head I was trying to send Ronald a message: "Don't tell her the truth. Don't tell her the truth. Don't—"

"To tell you the truth," I said, "we came to Capstone Island because we're looking for—"

"A sea monster," Julianne interrupted.

We all turned to her. Vivienne's mouth fell open, but Jeeves hid his shock like a pro. In fact, he was so calm that he looked ready to fall asleep. His eyelids drooped, and the corners of his mouth hung slack.

"I'm sorry . . ." Vivienne forced a little giggle. "Did you say *sea monster*?"

"Uh . . . yeah," Julianne said. "We heard that people sometimes see it around here. I think they call it . . . the *Serpent of the Mist*? Anyway, we were going camping and thought it would be fun to . . ."

She trailed off. Vivienne's eyes were sharp and cold. "Where did you hear this ridiculous story?"

"Oh," Julianne said, shifting in her seat, "from some crab fishermen who brought us here . . . for our campout . . ."

Vivienne was listening eagerly, but when I looked back to Julianne—

My head felt fuzzy. My eyes had started to blur. I looked into my teacup, then at Ronald. He was just a hazy shape.

"Abernathy?" Ronald said. "Madeline. Madeline! Are you okay?"

Who was Madeline? Was that my fake name? I licked my lips. I had to say something. The safety words!

"Grappling . . . cucumber . . . hook . . . sandwich . . ."

THUNK! Something Jeeves-shaped collapsed into a heap on the floor next to me. The teacups rattled in their saucers. I tried to stand. It took every ounce of strength I had. My legs were noodles.

Julianne staggered to her feet and slid the espresso filter out of her sleeve. "Rinnnnnnald," she slurred, waving the filter weakly, "weveeeeeee binnnnn poisinnnnned."

18

Poetry to the Rescue!

Julianne's eyelids started to fall closed as she tottered toward Vivienne. The poetess backed into a corner and snatched up an ivory letter opener. I sprang to my feet.

"It's only sleeping potion," Vivienne said, looking at my gasping adventure partner. "Kindfire said he'd take my house. I'd have nowhere to write poe-emmmms."

The espresso filter slipped out of Julianne's grasp, and she slowly slumped to the floor. I felt behind me and found an unstacked Russian nesting doll. I grabbed the two biggest dolls in the set.

"I had to do it," Vivienne said, her voice beginning to tremble. "Why aren't you sleeping, Feety?"

I glowered at her. "Because I'm *actually* master adventurer Ronald Zupan, which means I'm far too clever for such simple ruses. Especially when the host forgets to set out sugar."

Vivienne jabbed the letter opener toward me. "*Bill! Jake!*" she screamed.

I expected to hear the front door burst open, but nothing happened. My enemy's face grew desperate.

I reared back and threw the largest doll at her. She ducked, and it smashed against the wall. I threw the second doll and she dodged that too.

"*That was a gift!*" Vivienne screamed.

I kept reaching behind me for dolls, but they were getting smaller and smaller and the poetess easily leaped out of the way. By the time I finally hit her, it was with a doll the size of a thimble.

FACT: Our host was surprisingly quick on her feet.

Before I could grab anything else, Vivienne charged at me with her letter opener slashing through the air. I dodged back, around the table, but she kept coming—her silver hair flowing behind her. "*Drink the tea! There's no place like Hode!*"

I snatched up a cup and turned around to wing it at her. Just as I did, my foot snagged on something and I lost my balance. My rib cage bounced off the arm of a chair, and I landed in a heap on the floor, between my two sleeping friends. The satchel full of picnic supplies was right beside me, and the strap was tangled around my legs.

Our captor closed in, her eyes glinting like the steel of a cutlass. "You don't understand, I *need* this house. Now drink the tea and sleep."

The neck of the champagne bottle peeked out of the satchel, and I was struck by a moment of pure Zupanian brilliance. As Vivienne poured a fresh cup of her strange brew to put me to sleep, I snatched the bottle and tore off the gold foil that covered the cork. Then, when the dastardly villainess faced me again, I gave the bottle a violent shake and pressed the cork with both thumbs—

POP!

The cork rocketed toward Vivienne DuVoe and hit her right on the bridge of the nose. The teacup fell from her hand and shattered. She staggered backward, slipped on the spilled tea, and dashed out of the room, screaming for the Brothers Grin. I grabbed the neck of the champagne bottle, ready to give chase, when my eye caught on a better weapon.

On the floor, Vivienne's blue notebook rested in a puddle of spilled chamomile. I stooped to pick it up and instantly thought of one of my mother's famous sayings: "If you can capture one of a villain's most tender possessions, you can use it as tender to negotiate."

"Vivienne, I have your notebook!" I yelled. *"Come in here unarmed or it goes in the fire!"*

There was a pause, then a pained wail from upstairs. I opened the notebook to the first poem and started to read:

The tumbling of waves against the seashore is my favorite song,

Their rhythm stirs my memory, like a long-forgotten lullaby.

The salt air flirts with my senses and I breathe it in,

> ## *If anyone tried to take me from Hode House,*
> ## *I'd throw him off a cliff.*

"*I'm burning the first page!*" I yelled.

"No," Vivienne said. She was at the dining room door, eyes puffy with tears. "You win. Don't hurt my poe-*emmms.*"

"Sit," I ordered.

She crossed the room and slumped down in a chair, defeated. "You must hate poetry to ever threaten such a thing."

"I've actually had a taste for sonnets since I was just a boy," I said. "But you poisoned my friends."

Her expression was sullen. "I had no choice."

"Master adventurers always have a choice," I snapped. "Now, I need answers."

Vivienne shook her head violently. "I would be in far too much danger."

She snatched the only unbroken teacup, put it to her lips, and drank it down. She refilled it and drank again. The next time, she slowed down enough to look at me over the rim of her cup. "I drink to thee, Ronald Zupan."

Her body settled deeper into the chair and her eyes glazed over. I stepped toward her. "Who is Kindfire?"

Vivienne's face flooded with panic. "I said no such name. You misheard me."

"Where is Josh Brigand? What is the Serpent of the Mist?"

Vivienne slid out of her chair and down to the floor, a faint smile curled on her lips. "The potion is quick."

Her eyes fluttered closed. I stooped next to her to make sure she was out, then slipped the blue journal back in the pocket of her dressing gown.

Behind me, I heard Julianne mumbling in her sleep. She was already starting to stir. I turned around and saw her eyelids flutter. I raced to the sink for a glass of water and handed it to her. She smiled at me and I felt warm for the first time since diving off Delenda's boat.

"Sato, your adventure partner has rescued you!"

Julianne groaned and lifted her head. She saw Vivienne DuVoe on the floor, drooling on the Persian rug.

"Feel free to call me a dashing swashbuckler," I said. "Or a swaggering gentleman of fortune, or—"

I propped myself up on an elbow to look around the room. "Can you settle for a simple thank-you?"

"Deal," Ronald said with a smile, reaching out a hand to help me to my feet.

19

A Clean Escape!

I helped Julianne sit up, and explained how I'd escaped Vivienne DuVoe. She squeezed her eyes shut and leaned her head back against the mint-colored wall.

"Four sips," she muttered. "It took me four sips before I finally realized something was off."

"It was a sly trick," I said. "Jeeves had two full cups of the stuff."

Julianne angled her head toward Vivienne. "And her?"

The poetess was lying on the broken pieces of a Russian doll.

"She had three," I said. "She'll probably be out for a while."

"What about the Brothers Grin?" Julianne asked. "They never came back?"

Now that I slowed down to think about it, that part seemed

strange. Vivienne had told them they shouldn't be gone more than ten minutes. We let Jeeves rest and Julianne started to explore upstairs. I went out the back door and crept around the side of building.

At the corner of the house, I stopped, slowly leaning just far enough to see where the Jeep had been. The Brothers Grin were still gone. I looked around the property. There was a small shed and a clothesline crossing the yard.

Back in the kitchen, Julianne rushed up to me.

"I've got something," she said. "Look at this!"

She passed me a pink notepad, the same color as the paper Vivienne had given Bill Grin. The page was blank, but I didn't need an explanation.

As Helen Zupan always says, "Look closely at any pad your foe has written on. You might be impressed by how *in*-pressed the writing is."

I ran to Jeeves and rooted around in his jacket pocket. I knew he always had a pencil for doing the crossword puzzle. He even keeps a sharpener, in case his lead breaks.

I found the pencil and dashed back to Julianne. She gently rubbed it across the pad and words began to appear.

Strangers on island STOP

Two kids tall man STOP

Exited tunnels after FIB STOP

Sent Brothers Grin to collect STOP

Will bring to dock at sunset STOP

Now may I stay at Hode House forever

"This was the telegram Vivienne had the Brothers Grin send," Julianne said.

I reread the whole message again.

"Vivienne said the name 'Kindfire,'" I told her. "Then she tried to lie to me about it. This must be going to him."

Julianne nodded. The twists and turns of this side adventure sparked more questions than our combined deductive genius could handle. Why would this Kindfire have Vivienne poison us, unless he was working with the FIB?

How could he *not* be helping them? He had to be, right?

I thought of Josh. He'd been so nice to me since we rescued his ship in Borneo. When he found out my grandfather liked chocolate cake, he'd sent one to our house. When I mentioned that Ronald and I wanted to find my parents' lost ship, he offered to sail us down to South America.

And now he was in a dungeon somewhere . . . or worse. Because some FIB goon thought he was Jeeves. Because of us.

"We need to keep moving," I said, putting my hand on Julianne's shoulder. "The Brothers Grin will be back any minute."

"What about the fennec foxes?" Julianne asked. "We can't just run across the island."

"There's a shed in the back," I said, "maybe Vivienne owned an adventurous vehicle of some sort. Even something as slow as Jeeves's old motorcycle could help us now."

I dashed out the back door and sprinted to the shed.

FACT: There was no adventurous vehicle. Just an old gas generator mounted to a little pull cart.

I thought the generator's engine might be loud enough to scare the fennec foxes away, so I dragged the cart out of the shed. I pulled the starter cord and it came to life, purring like a Kenyan meerkat.

"We're going to need something louder," I said to myself.

I dashed into the house and found Julianne in the kitchen, rooting through Vivienne's cupboards.

"Sato, what are you—"

"A-ha!" She wheeled toward me, holding up a vial and shaking it. There was a slow-moving, silvery liquid inside. "The sleeping serum!"

"Excellent!" I said. "I found a cart—we just need a chair for Jeeves!"

"Like the ones in the dining room?" Julianne asked.

"Yes, without the legs!"

While Julianne broke a chair apart, I started searching the closets. I threw open one door, then another, but it wasn't until

I got to the coatroom that I found something loud enough to *really* scare the foxes: an old vacuum.

We dragged Jeeves outside, balanced the seat of a chair on the edge of the generator cart, and sat the butler down backward. Julianne tore down the laundry line and tied Jeeves and the chair in place while I carried our superb noise-making device from the house and plugged it into the generator.

Two minutes later, we were out the gate. We both dragged the handle of the generator cart with one arm. Any time a pack of fennec foxes came too close, I'd charge toward them.

The plan worked perfectly! The loud whirring of the vacuum kept the foxes away, and soon we were traveling as fast as two eleven-year-olds pulling a gas generator and a sleeping butler could possibly go.

We crested the top of a hill and the Hode House was suddenly out of sight. The sun peeked over the horizon in the east, shining down bright and clean after the storm. It was the sort of sunrise that made you feel hopeful.

"Well, Sato," I called over the noise of the vacuum, rushing to scare off another pack of the frisky foxes, "that was a neat exit, don't you think?"

She smiled at me. "A tidy getaway if I ever saw one."

20

Out Foxed!

We rolled down the back side of the hill into a small valley. Jeeves still wasn't stirring, even with the noise of the vacuum cleaner. I noticed that a few dozen foxes had formed a ring around us. They weren't edging close yet, but being surrounded was hard on the famous Zupanian nerves.

"Question," Julianne said, "what are we going to do when the generator runs out of fuel?"

"Fear not, Sato," I said. "By the time we——"

"Don't," she interrupted. "Every time you say something is going to be easy, catastrophe strikes."

"Sato," I said, "that's just superstition. The generator has however much gas it has and my being optimistic won't change that in the slightest."

It was a triumph of Zupanian logic, which I punctuated by scaring off a few curious fox cubs.

It's true. He made a solid point. And I might have even admitted that if the generator hadn't died at that very moment.

The second the vacuum stopped whirring, the foxes began to inch closer, trapping us in a dry little valley. I knew there were still two cans of anchovies left in the satchel, but those wouldn't buy us much time.

Ronald pulled the cord and the generator rattled back to life. The vacuum whirred and the foxes shrunk back . . . but not much. A minute later, the generator sputtered to a halt again. This time there was no starting it.

Dozens of foxes surrounded us. They dove over sagebrush and off rocks, closing in until they were only a few feet away.

"We can fight or run," I said, as the valley flooded with still more of the tiny animals, "except we have no weapons to fight with and nowhere to run to."

One bold fox dashed up to us, sprang onto Jeeves's lap, stared wildly around with bulging eyes for just a second, then leaped off and scampered back to the group. If there hadn't been so many of the things, and we hadn't seen Bill Grin's missing earlobe, it would have seemed absolutely adorable. But the bigger foxes noticed, and their circle tightened.

I pointed to the crest of the next hill, where a second pack of foxes bounced and scampered like they'd just set up camp on Nicaraguan fire ants.

Julianne took some matches and a fistful of sparklers out of the satchel. Meanwhile, I tore through my adventure journal looking for a tip. The only thing I found on the subject was a note scribbled in the margins:

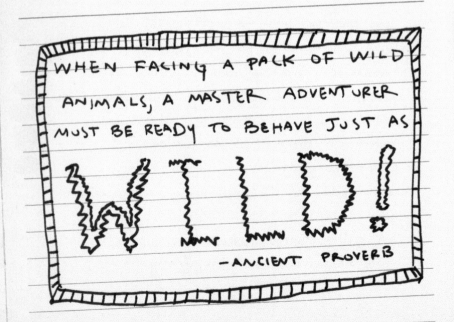

WHEN FACING A PACK OF WILD ANIMALS, A MASTER ADVENTURER MUST BE READY TO BEHAVE JUST AS

WILD!

—ANCIENT PROVERB

Without any better ideas, I started to growl and bark at the foxes, hoping to scare them off. The results were . . . *mixed.*

"*Waooo!*" I howled. "*Yawaooooooooooo!*"

"Ronald," Julianne called. She had the sparklers lit and was waving them frantically.

"*Wayawhoooooooooo!* What is it, Sato?"

"It's—"

"*WAYAAAHAOOOOOOOOoooooooooooo!*"

"Sssh! Listen!"

I paused for just a second and immediately heard the deep growl of a motor. It was close enough that I could also hear the tires churning up the hard dirt, just on the other side of the hill.

"It's the Brothers Grin," Julianne said. "They can save us!"

"*Save us?*" I asked. "By taking us back to a woman who drugged poor Jeeves here? By delivering us to this Kindfire, whoever *he* is?"

"We can handle the Brothers Grin," Julianne said as she chased away a fox that was gnawing on the sleeping butler's shoe. "On the other hand, I don't like our chances against this swarm."

She made a good point and her sparklers were burning out fast.

"What should we do?" I asked.

The sound had already started to fade again. The Jeep was headed the opposite direction. Julianne reached down and tore up a patch of desert sage. Holding it by the roots, she lit it off the sparklers and waved it so that a thin trail of smoke curled up into the sky.

"Help me send a signal!" she called.

Still capering around like a fox, I uprooted two more bushes and lit them off hers. They were dead, but still a little wet from the storm, so they gave off plenty of pungent smoke.

"Hopefully those ruffians see it," I said. "They didn't strike me as the observant type."

"Fingers crossed," Julianne agreed.

The foxes tightened their circle, yipping and barking at the fire. When the bushes burned down to their roots, Julianne and I dropped them and let them smolder. Sweat streamed down my forehead.

"*Where am I? What is . . . ? Why?*"

Jeeves had finally opened his eyes—only to find himself tied to a chair, perched on top of a generator, with two hundred fennec foxes closing in all around him.

FACT: It was not the easiest situation to wake up to.

"*Ronald!*" he yelled. "*Untie me! What are . . . ? What have . . . ?*"

"*Listen!*" Julianne cheered. "The Brothers Grin must've noticed the smoke!"

Sure enough, we could hear the engine roaring in our direction again.

Jeeves wrestled with the clothesline tying him to the broken chair. "*Why am I . . . ?*"

"It's simple," I said, "Vivienne drugged you but I defeated her, then we tied you onto this cart and dragged you away from the house using a vacuum to scare the foxes. It was going great until the generator ran out of fuel and the foxes circled closer, which is when Julianne decide to start a fire so that the Brothers Grin could recapture us!"

"And there they are!" Julianne yelled, jabbing her finger at the crest of the closest hill just as a Jeep launched off it, spraying dirt in all directions.

The foxes scattered, letting out a chorus of panicked squeaks. There was too much dust to see what was going on, but the Jeep bore down on us, then veered off, tore around the cart in a tight circle, and skidded to a halt, with the passenger door just a few feet from where Julianne and I stood.

"Except it's not the Brothers Grin," Julianne said, fanning away a cloud of dust.

"It's not? Who is it?" Jeeves asked, still fighting the knots that held him to the chair and trying desperately to turn around.

"It's me," Elias said, rolling down his window and flashing us a smile. "Because temporary members of the Danger Gang never forget a friend."

21
The Scientist!

Elias leaned out the window with a slingshot, stretched it back, and sent something rocketing into the distance. The last few fennec foxes raced after it.

"Dog snacks," he said to us with a smile. "The foxes love 'em."

The woman at the steering wheel was wearing a silk headscarf. By her high cheekbones and hazel eyes, it was easy to deduce that she was Elias's mother.

"Get in," she said, waving us toward the Jeep. "We'll take you back to the other side of the island."

I untied Jeeves and helped him to his feet. He was still feeling wobbly and his pupils were just two tiny pinpricks. Julianne opened the back door and we eased the battered butler into the middle seat.

No sooner had our doors closed than Elias's mom stomped on the gas and we sped away from the foxes, leaving the cart, the generator, and the vacuum behind.

"Elias you saved us," Julianne said. "We were fox food."

The woman in the headscarf turned halfway around. "You can call me Suraya. Elias has been going on about you three for hours." We hit a rock and the car bounced, but Suraya didn't even flinch. "Why don't you tell us how you came to be in an open field surrounded by two hundred foxes."

Julianne launched into the thrilling tale of chasing Josh Brigand's kidnappers down the tunnel, watching helplessly as they escaped in a boat, and meeting the Brothers Grin. When she got to the part about being drugged at the Hode House, I took over and explained how I'd hit Vivienne DuVoe in the forehead with a champagne cork and threatened to throw her journal in the fireplace.

"I know the name Kindfire," Suraya said, when I mentioned the name. "That's who hired me."

"What's he look like?" Julianne asked.

The scientist shook her head. "He only ever writes me. Every few days I wake up to find a letter pinned to the door."

"What do the letters say?" I asked.

Suraya pulled the wheel to the right to avoid a giant sage bush and glanced at me in the rearview mirror. "The last one

was strange . . . it wanted to know if there was a way to *train* the foxes."

The Jeep slowed down as we eased over the crest of a hill. Below us, the harbor lay flat and calm. The sunlight blinked off the wings of the Zupan seaplane.

"So how did you find us?" I asked.

Suraya tapped the gas and we started creeping down a steep, rocky decline toward the harbor. "Elias told me you'd gone in the tunnels, so we drove to the three exits that I know of. We saw the Brothers Grin in front of the first door we came to. Nice bit of work you three did on them."

Jeeves frowned. "Sorry . . . I'm still feeling a little out of sorts. What do you mean a 'nice bit of work'?"

Elias turned fully around in his seat. "The Brothers Grin were knocked out and tied up on the roof of their car. Did the Danger Gang do that so that the foxes couldn't get them?"

Jeeves and I looked at each other, baffled. Julianne was gazing out the window, deep in thought.

"We didn't see the Brothers Grin," I said. "Not after Vivienne DuVoe sent them away."

"Then who knocked them out?" Suraya asked.

We'd reached the bottom of the hill and were crunching across the gravel path in front of the harbor.

I shook my head. "I'm afraid that on this one rare occasion, Ronald Zupan is mystified. So is the rest of the Danger—"

"I know who it was," Julianne said.

I looked at her and she gave a little half shrug. "I saw someone, way back in Bay City, following us as we drove to the harbor. Then there was a boat, sailing through the storm behind us. Remember, I asked if you saw it? Then, just as we arrived at the caretaker's house, I saw her up on a ridge. She was wearing a cape."

"Did you say 'her'?" Jeeves asked.

"I'm pretty sure it was a her," Julianne said. "There was something about the way she moved."

Suraya was listening closely. "Another enemy?"

Julianne scratched the tip of her nose. "If she wanted to hurt us she could have come in the theater, or to the Hode House. But she didn't do either of those things. I think . . . I think she might be looking for Josh."

"That's good," Elias said, "right?"

I shrugged.

"Still . . ." Julianne wondered. "Who *is* she?"

We pulled alongside the dock. Julianne had given us a big reveal; now it was my turn. "Stop the Jeep."

Suraya hit the brakes and we skidded to a halt.

"Jeeves, didn't you tell me once that you knew how to hot-wire a car?"

It took a few seconds for the loyal butler to answer. "Well . . . Your father taught me when we were living in Rome . . . but I'm sure I've forgotten."

"You could at least try," I said.

"We don't even have wire cutters."

"I have three different types of wire cutters in the back," Suraya told him. "I'm working on a fence to keep the foxes out of the theater."

"Why do you want to get the plane started?" Julianne asked.

I straightened up in my seat, letting the spirit of adventure rush over me like a Maltese windstorm. "Whoever took Josh Brigand left this island in a boat. Whoever Kindfire is, the telegram said that his men will come to the docks in a boat. And the Serpent of the Mist—whatever *it* is—is out in the ocean somewhere too. We'll have a lot better chance seeing all three of those things from the air than by taking a boat of our own."

"Especially because we don't *have* a boat," Julianne added.

I faced Jeeves. "We need that seaplane."

Jeeves scratched the bridge of his nose. "I suppose it's worth a try."

Suraya locked eyes with me in the rearview mirror. "You

can't expect us to stay on an island full of kidnappers, poisoning caretakers, and strange women in capes."

Our eyes met, and I could see that this scientist was no one to be trifled with.

"You can help us," I said. "We need lookouts."

Elias's eyes lit up. "Because I'm a temporary member of the Danger Gang?"

"Indeed," I said. "Can we count on you to radio us if—"

"We're leaving this island," Suraya interrupted.

I started to argue but Jeeves put his hand on my arm to stop me.

"You're doing the right thing," he said to her. "It's not safe."

Suraya drummed the steering wheel for a second, then faced me. "We'll radio you if we see anything strange before we leave, but we aren't waiting here any longer than we have to."

"Radio Captain Delenda Jean-Baptiste," Julianne said. "She stays on channel 174. Tell her you're friends with Jeeves. She likes him best."

I watched as my dear butler's face slowly turned the color of a strawberry dart frog. "I'd . . . I . . . better try to hotwire that plane," he stammered. "Now is it green wires touch blue and yellow with . . ."

I got out of the Jeep to let him out. He opened the trunk, found the toolbox, and started across the waterlogged dock. Julianne and I hung back.

"If you see anything—" I said to Elias and Suraya.

"Before you leave, that is," Julianne added.

"We'll radio you right away," Elias said, glancing over at his mom.

Suraya didn't seem to be listening—something behind us had distracted her. I turned around. The propeller of the plane was already spinning. Jeeves stood tall next to it, wearing a broad smile.

"That was quick!" Julianne said.

"Wasn't much to it; the kidnappers left the keys in the ignition."

"Those FIB fools made it easy for us!" I cheered.

"Yeah," Julianne said, in a voice as dry as the Sahara, "what fools *to leave the keys inside.*"

Elias and Suraya waved goodbye and rumbled back along the harbor to the theater. Julianne, Jeeves, and I clambered aboard the plane.

I sat in the copilot's seat and counted back the hours since the kidnapping. The man on the radio had called himself "far more frightening" than the pirate Zeetan Z, and Zeetan Z had nearly killed the Zupans. What did that mean for Josh?

I couldn't stop imagining my friend locked in a cell somewhere, writhing in pain.

The FIB had probably dreamed up some horrible way to torture him.

Without noticing, I started biting the corner of my pinkie nail. Then rubbing my eyes. Then picking at the vinyl armrest to my seat.

   "We have to rescue Josh," I said to no one in particular. "And we have to hurry."

22
Flight Plan!

The ocean was glassy and the sun shone bright. I turned the plane and headed out of the harbor. As soon as we had some loft, I buzzed a wide circle over the theater.

"It was a long night and you were both drugged by a mediocre poet," I told my friends. "Get some rest."

"I thought the whole point was for us to look for suspicious activity," Julianne said. "Like a boat, or . . ."

"The Serpent?" I asked. "It doesn't sound like something I'd miss. We can fly in half hour shifts. As soon as I see something, I'll wake you."

I was too tired to argue and leaned against the window of the seaplane. The sun beat against the glass, warming my whole body. Maybe a little more rest would help me unwind some of the mysteries of Josh's kidnapping.

Soon, I started to feel sluggish, almost like when I'd drunk Vivienne DuVoe's tea. I let the hum of the propellers drown out my worries, soothing . . .

. . . me

. . . right

. . . to

s
l
e

e

p

While my friends napped, I piloted a lazy loop around the island. I wanted to pass the cliffs, to work my way northwest in the direction the boat carrying Josh Brigand had gone.

Guiding the plane with one hand, I took out my adventure journal to jot a few notes.

WHAT WE KNOW

⭐ JOSH BRIGAND WAS KIDNAPPED BY THE F.I.B., WHO MISTOOK HIM FOR JEEVES

→ SOME OF THE VILLAINS LEFT BAY CITY IN A BOAT, THE REST ABSCONDED WITH OUR SEAPLANE.

THEY LANDED AT CAPSTONE ISLAND, BROKE INTO THE OLD MOVIE THEATER, RAN THROUGH A SYSTEM OF TUNNELS, AND MET THEIR BOAT (OR ANOTHER BOAT?) AT THE BOTTOM OF A 200-FOOT-CLIFF.

WHAT WE DON'T KNOW:

o WHO IS KINDFIRE? WHY DID HE HAVE US POISONED?

o WHO IS THE WOMAN IN THE CAPE? WHAT DOES SHE WANT?

o WHAT IS THE SERPENT OF THE MIST? DOES IT REALLY SPIT FIRE AND WAIL LIKE 1,000 TERRIFIED SOULS???

The details of our side adventure knotted together and rolled around my brain like a spiny anteater. There was no making sense of them. I winged low over the ocean, looking for a boat, a sea monster, *anything*. All I saw was endless blue.

I flipped to a page in my adventure journal about the FIB, but it was practically blank. The name of their leader and the location of their hideout were unknown.

FACT: Ronald Zupan was completely stumped.

I puffed up my cheeks and let the air out slowly. I drummed my fingers on the controls of the seaplane. I tapped my chin exactly like my mother does when she's deep in thought.

That's when it hit me: *I could ask my parents!* They were probably worried sick about their beloved son anyway. I snatched the radio receiver and called Zupan Hangar. We were out of range, so I flew east toward Bay City until I could pick up a signal.

"Elexander," I said, hoping to catch our family's master mechanic, "do you copy?"

After a long pause, a voice crackled over the airwaves. "Ronald, where *are* you? Julianne's grandfather is worried sick."

"And my parents, too, probably," I said. "Can you patch me through?"

"Impossible," the master mechanic replied. "Last night

they got a lead on a man living in the desert who might have been seen with one of their artifacts—the Brasher Doubloon. They drove out to investigate."

I felt my eyebrows pinch together. "Well . . . Didn't they want to bring me?"

"You were at the movies," Elexander said. "What's going on? Did something happen? Did Jeeves get himself concussed again?"

I glanced into the back of the plane, where Jeeves was asleep on a pile of canvas. His mouth hung open wide enough to swallow a grapefruit.

"He's not concussed," I said. "About my parents . . . do you know where they went?"

"Neesy's Rare Treasures," Elexander answered. "Smack in the middle of Death Valley."

There was a buzz of static across the airwaves. I looked at Julianne and Jeeves to make sure they were still asleep, then down at the ocean below us. It was a calm blue sheet, not even broken by the white trails of froth that streak the surface after a boat tears past.

"Ronald," Elexander said over the static, "when your parents get back, should I tell them to come rescue you?"

The word "rescue" nipped at me like a fennec fox. I didn't want my parents to feel like they had to *rescue* me. I was Ronald Zupan, a founding member of the Danger Gang. I defeated Zeetan Z!

"Tell Julianne's grandfather that she's with me," I said.

"That's what he's worried about," Davidson replied with a chuckle.

I turned the nose of the plane south but still didn't see anything. "Tell him we're just on a side adventure."

The radio was silent for a second. "It's hard to hear. Did you say *side adventure?*"

"Exactly," I said. "Jeeves told me that's what my parents call it when an adventure seems like it's connected to the one before. I'm still trying to think of a better name. How do you like 'Spin-Off Shenanigans'?"

Davidson didn't reply for a long time and I wondered if we'd lost signal again.

"Or maybe 'Epilogue Escapades'?"

The radio crackled to life again. "A side adventure isn't a real thing."

"Jeeves said—"

Elexander cut me off. "In all my years, I've never heard your parents talk about side adventures."

I swallowed hard. We were at the very edge of radio range.

"Ronald, you can tell me if you need help. Understand?"

I flipped through my journal, found my father's rules for avoiding a second-adventure slump, and read through them again.

"Ronald . . . ?" Elexander asked.

"Avoid predicaments that feel familiar," I said. "Never take the easy way out."

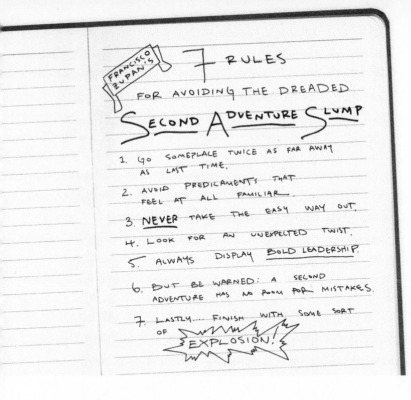

FRANCISCO ZUPAN'S

7 RULES

FOR AVOIDING THE DREADED SECOND ADVENTURE SLUMP

1. GO SOMEPLACE TWICE AS FAR AWAY AS LAST TIME.

2. AVOID PREDICAMENTS THAT FEEL AT ALL FAMILIAR.

3. <u>NEVER</u> TAKE THE EASY WAY OUT.

4. LOOK FOR AN UNEXPECTED TWIST.

5. ALWAYS DISPLAY <u>BOLD LEADERSHIP</u>.

6. BUT BE WARNED: A SECOND ADVENTURE HAS NO ROOM FOR MISTAKES.

7. LASTLY.... FINISH WITH SOME SORT OF EXPLOSION!

The radio sputtered and buzzed. "What?"

"Display bold leadership."

"Come in, Ronald," Elexander said. "I can't hear you!"

I hung up the receiver and lowered the nose of the plane until I was practically skimming the water. Then I circled higher and higher again, thinking through our situation.

- We were in a small seaplane instead of the huge cargo plane we'd flown to Borneo.

- We were circling an island not far from Bay City instead of exploring far-off jungles.

- We'd met a strange hermit, found secret underground tunnels, *and* had an adventurer knocked unconscious with a blow to the head—all things that had happened to us before.

> **FACT:** The Danger Gang was on a collision course with the second-adventure slump.

Then what? Maybe my parents would decide I wasn't cut out to go on their expeditions. Or Julianne and Jeeves would leave the Danger Gang. Or all the kids at Silver Hills Middle School would know that I'd failed as a master adventurer. Or . . .

I noticed how slick my hands were and wiped them on my pants. Far below I saw a school of tuna churning up the water until it looked like it was boiling.

I tried to think of something else—like my parents, off in Death Valley. Whatever lead they had about Neesy's Rare Treasures must have been good, or they wouldn't have driven out there so late.

"What sort of scalawag sets up shop in the desert?" I wondered.

Then another thought struck me: if this Neesy character had my parents' coin, and the coin was stolen by the FIB, then there was only one place this rogue could have gotten

it. Wouldn't that mean that he'd *also* know where the FIB's hideout was? And wouldn't that be where we'd find Josh Brigand?

My pulse quickened, and I drew another chart in my adventure journal:

COIN DEALER IN THE DESERT

FIB????

It wasn't much, but it was better than flying in circles. I glanced at my friends. They were both fast asleep. Julianne leaned against the window, her breath fogging up the glass. Jeeves muttered something about crumpets, tea, and a chess move called the Sicilian Defense.

Surely, they'd be fine with what I was about to do.

"After all," I said to myself, "trusting each other's hunches is part of the Danger Gang code."

I gripped the controls tightly. My parents were in the desert and it was time for an unexpected twist. It was time for bold leadership. I drew a deep breath, wavered for just a moment, then dipped the left wing of the seaplane.

We were headed for Death Valley!

23

Dry Landing!

"**Y**ou did what?" Julianne yelled.

She'd just woken up to find us soaring over the desert instead of the ocean, and the discovery had come as a bit of a shock.

My face broke into a broad grin. "Like Francisco always says, 'Luck favors the bold . . . and people who avoid hissing cockroaches!'"

"Ronald, you were supposed to circle the island, and now we're . . ." She peered down at the bone-dry earth. "Where *are* we?"

"Death Valley," I said. "I radioed Elexander and he told me about a man living here. My parents drove out to investigate this same shady character late last night. They think he might have a coin called the Brasher Doubloon that was stolen from our house by the FIB."

Julianne scowled. "Josh Brigand's kidnappers left in a boat! Why on earth would you go to the desert?"

I stole a glance at Jeeves, who was starting to stir at exactly the wrong time.

"*Well?*" Julianne pressed.

"The man in the desert," I said, lowering my voice, "if he knows about the coin, then he knows where the FIB is, right?"

"Why would the FIB tell some strange coin dealer where their hideout was?" Julianne demanded. "Did you even ask Elexander about someone named Kindfire? Or see what he knew about Capstone Island? Or . . . *anything?*"

I wet my lips and swallowed. My mouth suddenly felt bone-dry.

"That's great," Julianne said.

"I was displaying bold leadership," I mumbled.

Julianne shifted her whole body toward me. Her eyes flashed with anger. "You. Aren't. Our. Leader. We're a *team.*"

"I know that, but Ronald Zupan can still display—"

"That's the problem!" she exploded. "You still think you're the leader!"

I angled the nose of the plane down and we started our descent to the valley floor. "Sato, we have to trust each other's hunches. It's part of the Danger Gang code?"

Julianne shot me a look. "We don't *have* a code."

"Well . . . ," I said, "we *should* have a code. And trusting hunches should be part of it."

"But you didn't tell us about the hunch!"

An icy silence filled the plane. I didn't even bother mentioning it when I spotted Neesy's Rare Treasures beneath us. It stood alone on a dusty road, surrounded by tumbleweed, just like Elexander described. Behind it was a smooth stretch of desert.

A smooth stretch *without water!*

I wiped my hands on my pants. Clearly it was the desert heat that made me sweat, not the fact that we were trying to land in a dry valley.

While in a seaplane!

Luckily, it didn't seem like my adventure partner had noticed the—

Of course I noticed the landing situation. I just figured Ronald knew what he was doing.

I mean, who on earth would be crazy enough to fly all the way to Death Valley on just the thinnest shred of evidence and then try to land a seaplane on a dry lakebed?

"Ronald Zupan . . . breathe!" I said to myself, thinking of Helen Zupan's famous saying: "To make a plan before you have insight into your situation will only incite panic." Besides, my parents had a story about landing a seaplane on dry land in Mexico, so I knew it could be done. I just didn't exactly know *how*.

I eased off the throttle until the propeller was hardly spinning, and tried to gently touch down. It took four passes, but when our floats finally hit the valley floor it was as soft as the fur of a Peruvian chinchilla.

"Now seriously," I said, winking at Julianne as we plowed over a patch of purple desert poppies. "Was that not—"

CLANK!

One of our floats nicked a rock and the noise echoed through the cabin. Jeeves snapped awake.

"Where are we?" he said. "Where's Brigand? Did we find the FIB?"

"Not yet," I said, as the plane glided to a halt.

"Not yet?" Jeeves repeated, rubbing the sleep from his eyes. "Are we close?"

"That depends on how you define close," Julianne said, throwing off her seat belt. "Because Ronald wanted to show bold leadership—*so he flew us to Death Valley!*"

Jeeves sat up straight and peered out of a small window over the wing. "Oh, no Ronald . . . Can you please explain to me—"

I flicked off the engine and pocketed the key. "Explanations later; follow me!"

I took long strides toward the road and the lonely building sitting at the edge of the horizon. After twenty steps, I turned back. Jeeves and Julianne stood side by side, watching me with their arms folded.

FACT: Neither of them was following.

"Jeeves, I'll explain as we walk," I urged. "We have to find a man named Neesy, I have a hunch he can help us locate Josh Brigand!"

I was tempted to say "Juggy Brushbeard," but something told me it was bad timing.

Julianne shook her head. "This isn't a real hunch. It makes no sense."

"And you didn't tell us," Jeeves added. "It's deceptive, Ronald. You lied!"

I felt my face grow hot. Ronald Zupan doesn't get mad often, but when he does, he gets madder than a sugar badger who ate a pound of habanero chilies.

"Really?" I asked. "Because Elexander said you made up side adventures!"

Jeeves opened his mouth to speak, then hesitated.

"I *knew* my parents would call it something more dashing than that!"

"Fine," Jeeves said, shrugging, "I lied too . . . Because you cared more about a second-adventure slump than helping Josh!"

"What about you, Sato?" I said, wheeling on her. "You didn't tell us about the lady in the cape right away! Why's that okay?"

Julianne and Jeeves glanced at each other. Julianne lifted one shoulder, then dropped it again.

"First of all, you took us completely off the trail," she said. "And second of all, what we did was—"

"*Different?*" I yelled. "It's always different when you two do something wrong! And you always team up on me, even though *I'm* the one who introduced you!"

My fists were balled at my sides and I could feel a vein in my forehead throbbing. I spun away and started to storm off.

"Ronald, come back!" Jeeves called. "We need to talk about this!"

"No!" I yelled, stomping on a patch of sage. "I'm going to find this antique dealer! Kick me out of the Danger Gang, I don't care!"

Julianne cupped her hands around her mouth. "We need to rescue Josh!"

I kept walking, jamming my fists into my pockets.

"So you're leaving?" Jeeves yelled. "*You* were the one who said we stick together! That's a mutiny! You're a mutineer!"

I started to jog. Maybe it *was* a mutiny. Fine. All I could think about was getting to the building.

"You're being ridiculous!" Julianne called. "You don't even have water!"

"Ronald Zupan can survive for days without water!" I yelled over my shoulder, breaking into a full run. "Like a Gila monster!"

24

Neesy's Rare Treasures!

> FACT: Ronald Zupan *cannot* survive for days without water like a Gila monster. Not even close.

was too mad to think straight when I said that, but before I'd made it halfway across the valley floor my mouth was drier than the hoof of a Tunisian camel. Why hadn't I landed closer to Neesy's house?

The heat was sweltering. It crawled right down my throat. Still, I couldn't turn back. Not until I returned victorious.

After I was out of earshot, I slowed to a walk. I blinked the sweat out of my eyes and tried to focus on Neesy's Rare Treasures. The two-story home was still at least a mile away. In the distance, the heat radiated off the ground, making it look blurry.

My exhaustion from the night before hit me all at once, but the only thing to do was to take one step at a time— keeping an eye peeled for scorpions. As I plodded ahead, I wondered how Julianne and Jeeves were handling the heat back at the plane.

"More water?" Jeeves asked.

We'd found a ten-gallon jug in the cargo hold and both drunk our fill. We'd even poured a few cups over our heads to keep cool.

"I'm set," I said. I shook out the picnic blanket and spread it under the shade of an airplane wing.

Jeeves bit a chunk off one of our cheese wedges and passed it to me. "How long before we have to go after him?"

"Pretty soon, I think." I squinted into the distance. "It must be a hundred and ten degrees."

He chewed thoughtfully. "And he did come after me when I mutinied on our first adventure."

"In the meantime," I said, reaching for the cheese, "it's up to us to crack this case."

"Indeed," Jeeves said, sipping water from a tin mug.

"Josh isn't like the Zupans," I went on. "He can't handle being someone's captive. My grandfather and I were at his house last week, and he ran inside because of a bumblebee."

Jeeves chuckled and I paused to think for a second.

"There has to be something we're not seeing," I said. "What did that man say on the radio?"

Jeeves tapped his chin. "He said he was Ronald's archenemy. He said the trail to the Zupan relics was ice cold ... and ... and ... do you hear that noise?"

Now that he mentioned it, there was an odd droning sound coming from the opposite direction Ronald had walked. Almost like a giant swarm of flies, just on the other side of a sandy hill.

After listening to it for a full minute, Jeeves rose to his feet. "Francisco always says that loud buzzing should be investigated, in case it's a swarm of carpenter ants."

He started in the direction of the sound. "When I get back, what do you say we go find Ronald and make sure he's okay?"

My mouth was dry. My clothes were sticky with sweat, and my skin felt hot and puffy. I tried to catch my breath, but it was impossible—the heat had burrowed down into my lungs.

Finally, I reached the back of the house. It was surrounded by a ten-foot wall, painted light blue. I leaned a shoulder into it to keep from collapsing and staggered around to the front, where I found an unlocked gate made of twisted iron.

I swung it open and lurched toward the bright yellow door. On the doorframe was a brass knocker in the shape of a lion, and I clacked it three times, hard. Almost immediately, I heard footsteps tapping on stone; then the door flung wide.

"Cheerio, old chap." The voice came from a tall man with deeply tanned skin. He was on his tiptoes, looking like he'd just whipped a cape away from a charging Bolivian bull.

I was too thirsty to introduce myself with my trademark Zupanian flair. "I . . . came for . . . bold leadership . . . dramatic twist . . ."

The man settled down onto his heels and looked me up and down. "Blimey, sport, what seems to be the trouble?"

He had a British accent, but nothing like Jeeves's. It sounded more like Jeeves's rich uncle, Rollie Tottingham, who phoned Zupan Manor once a month.

"Come now, old egg," the man said, waving me in.

He had a slender face with high cheekbones, and his black hair was slicked back and shiny. He wore a purple silk ascot around his neck and didn't seem to feel the heat in the least.

"Could . . . something . . . drink," I gasped, ready to collapse.

"Right-o," the man said, and he whisked me inside. "A nip of water, that's the stuff."

A silver jug ringed with quivering water droplets waited on a marble table. The man poured me a glass and I drank it down in one gulp. He filled the glass again and I drank that one too.

"Jolly good show," the man said between my second and third glasses.

After the fourth, I straightened up. "You're very kind."

"Oh pish-posh," the man said, waving me off. "I'm only treating you like the spiffing fellow I'm sure you are."

I remembered why I'd come and looked past him, into the house's sunken living room. There was a Victorian couch upholstered in bright green fabric and an ornate table made of gold and glass. The fireplace was painted white, and the walls were covered with purple-and-gold wallpaper.

Above the mantel hung two skinny swords, called rapiers, crossed below a leather shield.

My parents were nowhere to be seen. Somewhere in the back of my head, it dawned on me that if they were still there, I would have spotted their silver coupe in the circular driveway.

"Come along, old boy," the man said, leading me down to the couch. "Rest your bean."

I followed him without thinking. I hadn't realized just how much I'd hoped to see my parents. Now that I knew they weren't still in Death Valley, the trip did feel sort of . . . *slightly less than crucial.* I crossed my fingers that Neesy had something vital to tell me.

"Beastly heat, isn't it?" the man asked. He set the pitcher of water down on the coffee table and slid into a blue velvet armchair.

I dropped onto the couch across from him. "A couple was here this morning, looking for the Brasher Doubloon."

The man's dark eyes focused on me and I cringed. If this stranger was in cahoots with the FIB, I'd already said too much. It made me wish I had Julianne by my side. She's an expert on knowing when to dodge questions from mysterious hermits.

My host crossed his legs. His socks were the same bright yellow as the door, with tiny blue anchors on them. "They left a half hour ago."

Now my thoughts flew to Jeeves. He was very finicky with grammar and those six words would have gotten under his skin like a deer tick.

"*How* long ago?" I asked.

"A half hour, old top," the man said. He reached a hand across the table toward me. "Come now, let's be mates. I'm—"

"Neesy, right?" I asked, peering closely at him.

He slipped his hand out of my grip and wiped it on his bright red trousers.

"Tell me, chap," he said, standing up, "why have you popped in?"

My host slowly took off his jacket and unwound his ascot. His movements were so elegant and I was so tired . . . it all felt like a dream.

The water pitcher rested between us on the coffee table. I poured myself another glass and held it to my forehead. When I looked up again, Neesy wasn't on the couch anymore.

I raised my head. The antique dealer had sprung—soft as a civet—onto the hearth and snatched one of the long, slender rapiers off the wall. His dark eyes glistened and he pointed the sword straight at me.

"Spiffing meeting this has been," he said with the tip of the blade dancing just a few feet from my chest. "But I'm not feeling so chummy all of a sudden."

25

The Brasher Doubloon!

I was sitting cross-legged under the wing again, flipping through Elias's book about the Capstone Company. Over the years, the island had been used for all sorts of movies, including four starring Josh Brigand. There was even a picture of him wearing a pith helmet and hiking through the valley where Elias and Suraya saved us, with a few fennec foxes scattered nearby. Underneath, the caption read, "Capstone Island stood in for the Sahara Desert in *Stranded in an Ancient Land*."

I snapped the book shut. There had to be something I wasn't seeing. Did it have to do with the woman in the cape? Who was she?

She'd seemed athletic. Brave, too. Could she be the piece that tied the whole case together? Trying to figure it all out made my mind feel dull.

"Sharp, isn't it?" Neesy said, admiring his sword.

I was helpless—sunk into the couch, with no weapon of any kind. Neesy's gleaming blade pointed right at my heart, which seemed to be pounding five times as hard as usual.

"Come now, old sport," he said. "How did you hear about the Brasher Doubloon?"

I swallowed the lump in my throat. There was another sword above the mantel. If I could just . . .

"I—I heard about the coin . . . ," I stammered.

Neesy rotated his wrist and the tip of the blade pressed into a button on my tuxedo shirt. *"From who?"*

I thought of Jeeves again. This last mistake was the sort of thing that would have made his eyebrows pinch together.

"Are you really British?" I asked.

The tip of Neesy's sword wobbled, and his arm slackened a little. I could breathe again.

"Of course I am!" he said. *"Why?"*

"You said the couple this morning left 'a half hour' ago,"

I said, never taking my eyes off the blade, "but a rich British person would have said, 'half *an* hour ago.'"

Neesy shook his head, but I could tell I was onto something.

"Then you said 'from who' instead of 'from whom,'" I went on.

My captor frowned, playing back his mistakes, and I saw an opening.

"We should ask my friends," I said, pointing past the rogue. *"They're right behind you!"*

Neesy wheeled around. No one was there, of course, but I'd bought myself a second. I somersaulted backward off the couch, then sprinted out of the room. I burst through two swinging doors and skidded into the kitchen.

Neesy swept into the room after me, sword dancing. He chased me around a small table, then the center island. He was long-legged and spry, and I was sure that I'd feel a sword tip against my spine at any moment.

As I raced past the refrigerator, I reached back for the handle and threw the door open. Neesy gave a grunt and I heard a glass bottle shatter. I glanced over my shoulder to see that his sword had speared the door. There were egg yolks dripping down like blood.

I bolted for the living room.

"You're a beastly cad!" Neesy yelled.

"Stop pretending to be British!" I yelled back.

I leaped up on the hearth and pulled down the second

rapier. It wasn't the same sort of sword Julianne and I normally trained with, but as the ancient saying goes, "There's no time to be choosy when you're trying to keep from being killed."

Neesy's razor-sharp blade entered the room first and the rest of him followed. He moved slowly, glowering at me, like a Peruvian panther.

"Well now," he said, "we'll jolly well see who the topper is, won't we?"

"I hope you fence better than you do fake accents," I replied.

We met in the middle of the room, swords clashing over the coffee table. Neesy fought like a dancer, swooping across the carpet, leaping over the couch, spinning past the hearth.

The crashing steel echoed in the cavernous living room. My opponent was a good fencer, but not good enough. Soon, I had him on his heels.

I slashed at his arm and he slipped, then sprang to his feet, backing away. I lunged for him and my sword snuck past his guard.

"You are spiffing with a sword," he said. "Absolutely spiffing!"

I doubled my intensity. I was tired and the life of a mutineer wasn't working out very well. I wished I had my friends by my side.

Attack, parry, riposte! Attack! Attack! ATTACK!

Enough of this, I thought. Josh Brigand was in peril, and

even if I believed that the actor was a talentless tree frog, my partner in dazzling schemes adored him.

Neesy lunged at me and I turned it. He charged at me again and I beat him back.

"*En garde!*" he roared, but I swatted him away like a Norwegian whisper moth.

"*En garde! En garde! En . . .*"

He made another frantic assault. I sidestepped it, then charged him, blade whistling through the air, until his back was pressed to the living room window.

"You probably don't even know the rules to cricket," I said.

I flicked my blade up, sliding it inside the knuckle guard of my enemy's sword, then forced it back down. His shoulders slumped as his rapier clanged to the ground.

We stood there panting, with the point of my sword leveled at his belly. After a few seconds, Neesy sighed.

"Fine, I'm not British," he said, passing a hand through his black hair.

FACT: His accent was completely gone.

"It gets lonely in the desert," he went on. "I have to keep myself entertained. Sometimes that means talking in strange accents, other times it means starting a swordfight with a boy because his parents said he out-dueled the leader of the Liars' Club."

I felt my whole body tighten up and raised the point of my rapier until it nearly grazed his Adam's apple. "What did you just say about my parents?"

Neesy smiled like a king cobra who'd just eaten a costume mustache. "I met them this morning. I pretended to be the Viscount of Transylvania, but they caught on right away. Turns out they *know* the Viscount of Transylvania."

I kept my blade steady. "Tell me everything."

Neesy gave the sword a wary glance, then stepped out from behind it and strode over to the couch. I let him go but kept my guard up.

"They came asking about the Brasher Doubloon, too," he said, plopping down and weaving his fingers together behind his head. "Once they knew I couldn't help them, they asked for a quick tour of my collection. When they saw the swords and the buckler—that's what the leather shield is called, you know—they told me all about you and Zeetan Z."

I frowned. "But how did you know it was me?"

Neesy smiled. "They insisted on showing me an article about you."

I felt a surge of pride ripple through my body and drank a sip of water to calm down. "Why couldn't you help them with the Brasher Doubloon?"

Neesy reached across the coffee table and snatched his smoking jacket off the blue velvet chair. He slipped a hand into the inside pocket and drew out a golden coin, a little bigger than a silver dollar. After holding it up for a moment, he flipped it up into the air. It spiraled high overhead, and he caught it by slapping it onto the back of his free hand.

"What's that?" I asked.

"The Brasher Doubloon, of course."

Neesy held his hand toward me, and I took a few steps closer. The coin was slightly misshapen, but I could make out a mountain with a sun rising just over the peak. In front of the mountain there were a few rows of waves.

My host tapped the coin with one finger and it flipped over. The image was an eagle with a shield on its chest. On the left wing there was a stamp: "EB."

"Those initials are the mark from the coin maker," Neesy said, making the coin waterfall across his knuckles. "Ephraim Brasher. When your parents saw that mark, they knew their trip was a waste."

I bulged my lip with my tongue, the same way Jeeves did when I asked him to help me build a hang glider out of bed sheets.

"Ephraim Brasher made two types of doubloon," Neesy explained. "This one, with the stamp on the wing, and the one your parents had stolen from them, with the stamp on the chest. Theirs is far rarer than mine."

If Neesy was telling the truth, it all fit together. My parents would have known, the second they saw this version of the Brasher Doubloon, that it wasn't theirs. Which meant that their trip to the desert had been a wild-goose chase, and my trip had been a wild-goose chase *of* a wild-goose chase.

"But you could have *both* coins," I said, after a pause.

Neesy leaned his head back. "Do I smell like a member of the FIB?"

He had a point.

"What else did my parents say?"

"They gave me this." The antique dealer dug into his jacket pocket again and took out an article cut from a newspaper. I recognized it right away.

BAY CITY RESIDENTS THWART GANG OF PIRATES IN BORNEO!

"Then I said to the pirate king, 'No, slithering sea devil!'" Ron City Gazette. "De

I had the same picture tacked up on my wall back in Bay City, but somehow seeing it at Neesy's, after mutinying from my friends, it looked . . . *different.* I folded the clipping up and handed it back.

"What about the Serpent of the Mist?" I asked. "Did my parents mention it?"

Neesy poured himself a glass of water and drank it down. "We don't get much mist in the desert."

"And Kindfire?"

He stared blankly at me. "Kind what?"

"Kind*fire.*"

Neesy studied my face for a moment, drumming his fingers against the armrest of his chair. "I met a victim of the FIB once, you know. This man, they left him with no water, about five miles from here."

"They're nowhere near as bad as Zeetan Z," I said.

Neesy shrugged. "The man they left in the desert . . . when I found him, his lips were cracked and bleeding. His skin was the color of a fire engine."

I tried to laugh, but it stuck in my throat.

"Just be careful," Neesy said, pocketing his coin. "The FIB might be more dangerous than you and your parents realize."

I stood up to leave. It wouldn't be fun explaining to Julianne and Jeeves that they'd been right about our trip to Death Valley. I needed *something* to make it seem worthwhile.

"Any chance you'd part with those swords and that shield?" I asked. "My friends and I need weapons."

My host thought about it for just a second, then his dark eyes gleamed. When he spoke, the snobby British accent was back. "I do say old boy, 'tis a spiffing idea. These swords are yours . . . *if* you can out-duel me again."

I nodded and he raced to pick up his rapier. "En garde, dear chap. *En garde!*"

26

A Titanic Hunch!

I ran back across the valley floor with a sword in each hand, the leather shield slung on my left arm, and a canteen full of ice water slapping against my side.

"Sato, I brought you a blade!" I called as soon as I got within a hundred feet of the plane.

I ran straight up to her and held out one of the rapiers.

"So," Julianne said, slicing the sword once through the air, "did you discover a vital clue and now the whole case fits together like an ancient Egyptian jigsaw puzzle?"

I could see that she was still on edge and decided to tread lightly.

"Helen once said . . . ," I was panting to catch my breath. ". . . 'Sometimes figuring out which clues are weak can take more than a week.'"

Julianne looked unimpressed. "Meaning?"

"In just a few hours, we figured out that Neesy wasn't important to our mission. *And* we got swords!"

My adventure partner let out a puff of breath. She looked ready to say something, but we were interrupted by a strange buzzing sound as a whole swarm of mismatched motorcycles came tearing over the lip of a nearby hill. Jeeves stood on the foot pegs of one of the vehicles with the wind playing through his wispy hair.

The whole crew skidded to a dusty halt, forming a half circle about ten feet from the plane. They wore goggles and leather helmets. Jeeves hopped down and crunched across the dry ground toward us, beaming like a wide-mouthed gecko.

"Ronald, glad to see the mutiny is over," he said, waving a polo mallet. "These men and women make up the Death Valley Motorcycle Club—they were riding just over that berm."

A few of Jeeves's new friends revved their engines.

"They were playing *polo*," he added, holding the mallet toward us. "On motorbikes!"

FACT: Polo is my dear butler's fifth favorite activity—after cricket, chess, telling me that swinging from the chandelier is a bad idea, and drinking tea.

"Anyway," Jeeves went on, spinning the mallet in his hand, "I thought they might tow us across the desert, to get the plane up to flying speed." He paused and eyeballed me. "That is, *if* we landed without knowing how to get aloft again."

"A big 'if'," Julianne said. "Ronald, you *definitely* had a plan for getting back in the air, right?"

I gulped, looking from Julianne to Jeeves.

"Jeeves," I said.

"Yes?" my butler asked, eyes twinkling a little.

"Do you think . . ." I hesitated. "Maybe . . . you could introduce me to . . . your friends?"

Ten minutes later, we were headed west. As soon as we were at altitude, I told the story of my meeting with Neesy. Jeeves and Julianne seemed to agree that getting attacked with a sword and putting up with a fake British accent were punishment enough, and started acting friendly again.

By the time Jeeves told us about playing umpire during

the Death Valley Motorcycle Club's polo match, my mutiny was a distant memory.

"What about you, Sato?" I asked. "What did you do on our little jaunt?"

My adventure partner gave a half shrug. "Tried to figure out who the woman in the cape might be, ate some cheese, and flipped through the book about the Capstone Company."

"Discover anything?"

Julianne shook her head, riffling the book's pages. "Not really . . . I guess the trail is ice cold just like . . ."

Her mouth fell open.

"What is it?" Jeeves asked.

I could tell that some idea had struck my adventure partner like a thunderbolt.

"I . . ." She hesitated for a second. *"That's it!"*

I could practically see the dizzying deductions coming one after another.

"What's *it?*" Jeeves asked.

"Ice cold," she said. "I know where we need to go next."

I started flipping through the pages of Capstone Motion Picture Company: The First 30 Years. The book was divided up with one chapter for each Capstone movie.

"The Liars' Club and the FIB always leave clues, right?" I asked my friends, nose deep in the book. "And the man on the radio said that the trail to the Zupan relics is ice cold."

I found the page I was looking for and held it toward Jeeves and Ronald. "Well, look at this!"

The spread showed a black-and-white photo of some sort of man-made iceberg floating in the water. It was a movie prop—with a bunch of men milling around on top. Below, there was a caption.

Crews work to finish the sets for *The Sinking of the Titanic!* which was both a critical and commercial failure.

Page 296 — *Capstone Motion Picture Company: The First 30 Years*

"See!" I said. "I think the Zupan relics are *literally* in the tip of this iceberg! It's ice cold, get it?"

Jeeves was at the controls and had the plane on a nice, steady course, so it was easy for him to lean over for a closer look at the picture.

"But that's so small," he said. "Are you saying that this is the FIB's hideout? You think their whole crew is there? Floating inside this iceberg? *With* Josh Brigand?"

Julianne looked annoyed. "Jeeves, icebergs keep most of their mass underwater!"

She turned to me for a reaction.

"Sato," I said, "if this fake iceberg is still in the water somewhere, wouldn't we have seen it when we were looking for boats?"

Julianne's eyes narrowed. "We might have if we hadn't flown to Death Valley for no good rea—"

"On second thought," I said, "let's investigate. You might be onto something!"

"Good," Julianne said, as we passed through a dense cloudbank. "Because without the iceberg, our hopes of finding Josh Brigand are sunk."

As soon as the seaplane was on course for Capstone Island, Ronald announced that he was going to take a nap. Actually, he said, "Rest my weary eyelids and recharge the dazzling Zupanian brain," but you get the point. There was a hammock slung so low that it brushed against the floor of the plane, and he plopped down into it and fell asleep in seconds.

"It's an interesting idea, with the iceberg," Jeeves said, sitting at the controls. "You always do astound me."

I turned to look out the window. "Actually, I've been feeling like maybe I'm having a bit of a second-adventure slump."

Jeeves didn't answer, just adjusted the seaplane's altitude a little.

"I mean, the FIB hardly seems to know I exist," I went on. "And Ronald was the one who had the final battle with Zeetan Z in Borneo, not me. I even fell for Vivienne DuVoe's trick. I think that's why I didn't say anything about the woman in the cape for a while . . . I wanted to figure out who she was by myself."

Jeeves's eyes crinkled.

"What?" I asked.

"So you were trying to be impressive?"

"Well," I said, bristling, "last adventure I was always a step ahead."

Jeeves chuckled. Maybe a few seconds too long, if you ask me.

"Julianne," he said, "when we were in Borneo, you told me you thought I was the best butler ever, do you remember?"

I nodded.

"Well, consider this: when Ronald was one year old, Elexander went on a vacation. At that time, we were close friends and he asked me to take care of his pet cobra."

"Carter?" I asked.

Jeeves smiled. "Back then the snake was

named Ellsworth, but yes, it's the same one. It kept biting me, so eventually I stored it in my bathtub and just decided to use a different restroom until Davidson retrieved the beast."

"And?"

"It escaped, of course. It crawled into Ronald's crib and attacked him." He paused. "You still fancy me a good butler?"

"Yes," I said. "One mistake doesn't change . . ."

I trailed off when I saw Jeeves chuckling. "And *that's* my point. You can be good—or even great—and you're still not going to be perfect."

I looked down at the new sword Ronald had given me, tracing a finger along the hand guard.

"We all need each other," Jeeves went on. "I know we need your help very much. You might need mine, too. Ronald *clearly* needs help from both of us and . . ." He looked into the back of the plane. "I suppose we need help from him sometimes."

I didn't answer, but I felt my jaw unclenching, millimeter by millimeter. Below us

the desert had given way to cities bustling with people. They zipped in and out of traffic and sat on park benches reading their morning newspapers.

"Of course," Jeeves added after a moment, "we can't tell Ronald we need him. It would go straight to his head."

I laughed. "Most definitely not."

The buzzing of static on the radio dragged me out of my slumber.

"What do you *mean* he's with the Zupans?" Julianne said. "He's eighty-five years old!"

There was another loud buzz, then Elexander's voice crackled across the radio waves. "The Zupans think you three were captured by the FIB. There was a ransom note in the afternoon newspaper. They went to rescue you."

"And how did my grandpa get involved?" Julianne asked.

"Well," Davidson said, "I called him and told him you were helping Brigand, just like Ronald said. But when the ransom note hit the newspapers, he saw it. Francisco and Helen said he was on their doorstep when they arrived from Death Valley."

I clambered out of the hammock and pulled the crate up between my friends. They were looking at each other, clearly concerned.

Julianne pressed the button on the radio handset. "Didn't *you* know we weren't captured?"

There was more static. "I couldn't get ahold of you either."

Julianne scowled. "Because we were out of radio range. *In Death Valley!*"

I reached for the receiver. "So where are my parents, Elexander?"

The radio sputtered—we'd flown past Bay City and were close to losing signal again. "They're headed to Capstone Island. That's the last location you gave me. You have the seaplane, so they took the speedboat."

The master mechanic was talking about an old mahogany boat that my parents kept under a canopy in a little harbor just south of Bay City. The boat was sleek and fast, but there was one major flaw.

"It doesn't have a radio," I groaned.

Julianne and Jeeves both turned in their seats.

"I took it out three days ago, so that I could have a radio in my bedroom. I wanted to be able to reach my parents at all times."

"Bitter irony," Jeeves muttered. He took the radio receiver from me. "So what exactly did this ransom note say?"

Elexander's voice hummed to life again. "The FIB wants Helen and Francisco to rescue the three of you, and Josh Brigand."

There was so much static across the airwaves that I

thought we'd lost the signal again, then Davidson's voice crackled to life once more.

"The problem is, the note didn't say *where* to rescue you. It just said you need to be rescued by tomorrow night. Or else . . ."

There was a long pause as the plane soared over water.

"Or else *what?*" I asked.

Davidson's voice came almost too scrambled to make out.

"Or . . . never . . . see . . . again."

28
The Worst of the Best of the Worst!

We were too far from Bay City to get a signal and the line went dead. Julianne reached over to click off the radio. Her features were drawn and serious.

"So, let me get this straight," she said, speaking slowly and measuring out every word, "the FIB thinks they have us captured . . . because of Vivienne DuVoe? And they want your parents to rescue us?"

"It's strange," I said. "She *must* have told this Kindfire that we escaped by now, right? And if he's connected to the FIB . . . which he *must* be . . ."

"Maybe the ransom note was sent to the newspaper before they found out?" Julianne said. "But it still doesn't make sense. Why didn't the FIB leader just have *you* kidnapped at the movie premiere, if he thinks you're his archenemy? Or kidnap your parents? Or ask for money? I just don't get his . . . *motivation*. What does he want?"

I shook my head. "They're dolts, Sato. If the Liars' Club calls itself 'The Best of the Worst,' the FIB motto should be 'The *Worst* of the Best of the Worst.'"

We all mulled over my clever wordplay in silence. After a long moment, Jeeves pressed his lips together—the same way he does every time I challenge him to a lively bout of Brazilian capoeira.

"Unless," he said.

Julianne and I both looked at him.

"Unlessssssssss," he repeated, drawing the word out.

"Out with it," I said.

"Yeah, what are you 'unless'-ing about?" Julianne asked.

Jeeves's features shifted rapidly, like an Ecuadorian alpaca eating spicy food for the first time. He motioned for me to take the seaplane's controls and I slipped into the pilot's seat. Next, the good butler crawled toward the back of the plane. His tuxedo jacket lay crumpled in a corner and he snatched it up, plunging a hand into the breast pocket.

"Jeeves, is that an adventure journal?" I asked when I saw him holding a black leather notebook. "Sato and I are really rubbing off on you."

He crawled back toward us. "For the past few weeks I've been spending my days off with Elexander down at Zupan Hangar. We were good mates once and we've taken up a friendship again."

"So . . . ," Julianne said.

"So, he showed me a chart the Zupans made about how someone takes control of the Liars' Club."

Jeeves started flipping through his adventure journal, and his face fell. "Oh . . . I . . ."

He held the notebook toward us. The pages were covered with runny splotches of black. The words were blurred and blotted.

"You forgot to use India ink," I said.

"Which is the only suitable choice," Julianne added.

Jeeves kept flipping through the waterlogged notebook. The pages he was looking for were stuck together, and he had to slowly peel them apart.

How a New Leader of the Liars' Club Is Chosen

1. The new leader must defeat everyone who defeated the old leader, in dramatic fashion.

2. While avoiding the mistakes that the old leader made.

3. Without showing any mercy. The Liars' Club needs a leader who is not afraid to spill blood.

"See entry number one?" Jeeves asked. "You can still make it out."

Julianne and I nodded.

"What if *that's* all the FIB leader is trying to do with all this: to defeat everyone who defeated the pirate Zeetan Z in Borneo and take over the Liars' Club."

"I'm not sure I follow you," Julianne said.

"If his master plan is to lead the Liars' Club, he'd have to defeat *all* of us, 'in dramatic fashion'—even if he only calls Ronald his archenemy. Then it doesn't matter if he captured one of us, or Josh Brigand, or . . . *whoever*. As long as the person he captured is worth the others trying to rescue!"

"Okay," I said, pulling back the plane's controls to raise the nose. "So are you saying he doesn't *care* if my parents think we're captured?"

Jeeves looked as excited as an over-caffeinated lemur. "It would be easier for him if they think we're captured. And maybe they do, maybe *he* still does. But it doesn't *truly* matter."

I'm nowhere near as experienced as Jeeves and Julianne at using my eyebrows to look skeptical, but I gave it my very best.

"Whether he thinks we're captured or not," the butler said, "whether your parents believe him or not—the FIB leader feels sure that we'll still try to help Josh Brigand and the Zupans will still try to help *us*."

We broke through a cloudbank and Capstone Island came into view. Slowly, I started to see where Jeeves was going with this.

"I don't think the FIB leader wants jewels or relics or even money." He paused for a moment. "I think all he wants is a showdown at his hideout, so that he can defeat us and take over the Liars' Club."

Jeeves held out the journal and we peered at the next two entries. With a little effort, we could make out most of what was written, except for a few words.

"But look at this last line," I said. "I find it hard to worry about a villain who would live by this code: 'Not afraid to spill food.' The Liars' Club and FIB really take pride in being slobs, don't they?"

I looked at Jeeves but he was watching Julianne. Her face was pinched with worry, like a meerkat stuck in a den of mambas.

Ronald was reading the smudged word wrong. I knew it, and I could see that Jeeves knew it too. I had a sour taste in my mouth, and my skin prickled.

"That's not what's written," I said. "It says 'The Liars' Club needs a leader who is not afraid to spill *blood*.'"

"*Exactly,*" Jeeves agreed. "Whoever this mysterious leader is, he's drawing us all to his hideout . . . but he doesn't expect us to leave alive."

29

The Tip of the Iceberg!

"**E**lias," I said, spinning the radio dials, "come in Elias."

We'd been looking for the floating iceberg for an hour and tempers were running high.

"I'm here!" Elias said. "Sorry, my mom and I were down in the tunnels!"

"Any news to report?" Jeeves asked.

"Yes!" Elias said. His voice sounded high-pitched across the radio waves. "We found costumes, like from the old movies that were filmed here. And props too. There was a bunch of swords. Didn't you say something about needing swords?"

I took the radio receiver. "We actually made a quick jaunt to . . . get some. In the desert. Did you find anything else?"

There was a pause filled with buzzing. "Oh, there was a

whole room full of paints and paintbrushes! Mom thinks they were for designing backdrops and sets."

I tapped my tongue against the roof of my mouth. So far, nothing Elias and Suraya had found sounded too promising. Jeeves didn't look very impressed either.

I knew Ronald and Jeeves weren't feeling too sure about my "tip of the iceberg" theory. Truthfully, I wasn't so sure about it anymore either. An hour of looking without any results will shake anyone's confidence.

But something Elias said started pinballing around my brain. Something about the rooms underneath the island.

"A whole room full of paints and paintbrushes."

I repeated that to myself a few times. The more I thought about it, the more important it seemed.

Ronald looked over at me from the pilot's seat. I could feel the edge of my lip curling in a smile.

"Elias, we'll call you back." He clicked off the radio and waited for me to say something.

"They painted the iceberg," I whispered.

Jeeves frowned. "What now?"

"The iceberg is a movie prop," I went on, speaking slowly so I could work everything out in my head. "If they wanted to hide it, they'd paint it blue, to match the water. That's why fisherman don't talk about it and why we haven't seen it."

Jeeves looked at Ronald first, then me. He tapped his chin a few times. "If that's the case, sunset might be our only chance to find it. The water will reflect the red of the setting sun, and the iceberg won't match. After that, it'll be too dark to see anything."

He paused. "Of course . . . sunset is also when Vivienne DuVoe was supposed to deliver us to Kindfire at the docks near Hode Point. And that must have something to do with the FIB, mustn't it? If the person who wrote the note thinks we're captured, he must have heard that from Vivienne."

"What are you saying?" I asked.

"If we go to the docks it might be a chance to surprise the FIB."

"But Vivienne might have called the

whole thing off," I said. "After all, we escaped. We might fly all the way there for nothing, then we couldn't find the iceberg."

Jeeves and I pondered it for a few minutes in total silence.

Ronald had been piloting the plane without saying a word, and after a while, I slowly turned to look at him.

"Well?" I asked.

"Well what?" Ronald said with a wink. "Sato, it's like I said: the Danger Gang trusts each other's hunches. It's part of our code. Or at least it should be."

We all saw the fake iceberg at the same time. Sure enough, it'd been painted blue and was easy to spot with the rest of the ocean reflecting the peach color of the sunset.

Right away, I started circling for a landing. Five minutes later, we'd touched down and the seaplane was gliding toward the massive movie prop. "What's our theory here?" I asked my friends. "Are we about to face the whole FIB?"

Julianne eyed the iceberg, "It *does* look kind of small in person. It seems like it would be a pretty cramped hideout."

"Still," Jeeves said, swallowing a lump in his throat, "it might be some sort of outpost, containing five or six merciless cutthroats. Which is still a few too many for my taste." The seaplane glided to a stop about ten feet from the iceberg. We crouched on the floats and paddled the rest of the way with our hands. The water was cold and gave me a jolt of energy.

Stepping off the plane, Julianne and I grabbed our swords. Jeeves belted the leather shield onto his forearm and picked up the Death Valley Motorcycle Club polo mallet.

"The problem," I whispered, "is that the FIB is secretive. They aren't likely to just announce their devious plans by—"

FACT: I was interrupted by the sound of the FIB announcing their devious plans.

"Francisco and Helen Zupan," came a heavy, thudding voice. "This is Deadly Dirk Grimple, second-in-command of the FIB, and assistant to your son's archenemy."

I just about to fire off a witty retort when a voice like a foghorn piped up.

"What are you doing, Deadly Dirk?"

We could hear the whine and fuzz of a radio inside the iceberg.

"Trying to get the parents of the boss's archenemy on the radio. Boss gave me four clues, and I'm supposed to give them one every eight hours. If they solve them, they'll find the hideout by tomorrow night. Then the boss will capture them, too—it's all part of the master plan."

There was a long pause inside the iceberg.

"Why is the master plan so confusing?" the voice asked.

Jeeves climbed up one side of the structure and leaned down to inspect something. He waved Julianne and me toward him. There was an air vent cut into the wood, and Dirk Grimple's voice echoed out of it.

"It's *not* confusing," the scalawag insisted. "Tonight the FIB hideout is open for business—half of Bay City is going to be there. But the only business tomorrow night is to defeat the whole Danger Gang, all at once. In dramatic fashion."

The vent was impossible to see through, so it didn't help us much. We still had no way to know how many people were inside the iceberg.

"What if they don't figure out the clues?" a third voice asked Deadly Dirk. "Then what will the boss do?"

"Stop asking questions," Grimple grunted.

He tried to call for my parents across the radio again. He prattled on about his boss and how Julianne, Jeeves, and I had been caught by the poisoning poetess at the Hode House. Little did he know that we were only a few feet away.

"*No answer!*" the villainous voice boomed through the vent. "If only I'd kidnapped Zupan's *real* butler at the movie premiere, I wouldn't have to do this job. That's why the boss stuck me here with you two numbskulls!"

"I'm not a numbskull!" the second man said. "And the only reason Brett can't feel his head is his hair-growth treatment."

"*Shut it, Dave!*" Grimple yelled.

A muffled whine echoed through the vent. The noise was high-pitched and trembling.

"That must be Brigand!" I mouthed to my friends.

"And guess what else?" Deadly Dirk yelled. "I've had it with this scurvy dog! Time to punish him!"

"Oh, Dirk," the third man cried, "don't! The boss won't want that! *Please!*"

"The boss only cares about the people who defeated Zeetan Z!" the murderous rogue boomed. "I could feed this ugly hellhound to sharks and he wouldn't mind a bit!"

I turned to my friends again. "He's going to hurt a beloved movie star!"

We tiptoed across the wooden surface of the fake iceberg, looking for a way inside. Jeeves found the entrance first and motioned us toward him with his polo mallet. There was a circular hatch, which could be opened only by turning an iron wheel.

We all gripped it and started turning it to the left.

"As silently as possible," I said. "The element of surprise is crucial for any rescue mission!"

30

Room Full of Ruffians!

SC
RE
EE
EE
EE
EE!

"Do you think they heard that?" I asked my friends as the hatch to the iceberg screamed with each quarter turn.

SC
RE
EE
EE
EE
EE!
CREEEEEEEEEEEEEE

Julianne looked at me, sweat running down her forehead. "Unless everyone inside is completely deaf, I'd say the
element of—"

SC
RE
EE
EEEEEEEEEEEEE

"surprise is—"

SC
REEEEEEEEE

"just about off the—"

REEEEEEEEE....
EEEEE.... ....
.... EE

"table." She wiped the sweat out of her eyes with the back of her arm.

The wheel had finally loosened up, and we spun it freely until we could swing the hatch open. I looked through the porthole and saw a ladder. By my best Zupanian estimate, the floor of the fake iceberg was ten feet down.

"Who's there?" Dirk Grimple roared. "Boss, I can't find the Zupans on the radio!"

Julianne, Jeeves, and I peered inside the iceberg just as a barrel-chested villain walked right under the opening of the hatch. It was Grimple—I recognized him at once. He was looking up, but with the sun setting behind us, I knew we'd be silhouetted.

"Sato," I whispered, "are our great minds thinking alike?"

My adventure partner smiled. "Indeed."

"One, two . . ."

"*Three!*" Ronald and I launched into the air, right at Deadly Dirk. In that split second, I could see the expression on his face turn from surprise to dread to . . . well, pretty horrible pain when two members of the Danger Gang landed right on his head.

Grimple collapsed under us and thudded against the floor of the iceberg. For just a moment our eyes met, then his pupils dilated and his body went limp.

Sato and I sprang to our feet with our swords whistling. Jeeves hopped down off the ladder and stood between us. He held his shield high and swung his polo mallet menacingly. The three of us stood over Dirk Grimple with no idea what

to expect. Were we about to face a room of ruffians? A sea of scalawags? An iceberg of ignoramuses?

"Uh . . . what did you do to Dirk?" a thick voice asked. It was clearly one of the men Grimple had been bickering with.

I peered into the farthest reaches of the dim room to see a man walking toward us out of the shadows. His long, greasy hair spilled from under a red stocking cap. "Hey! You three are supposed to be captured already. You're the . . . *you're*—!"

"The Danger Gang," I said, slicing my sword dramatically.

Directly in front of us, a shortwave radio and a telegraph machine sat on a workbench, buzzing softly. A deflated orange life raft was crumpled on the floor and six or so lanterns hung on hooks, casting flickering light. Like so many dens of villainy, the whole place had a certain sulfury smell to it.

"We're here to rescue Josh Brigand," Julianne said, rolling back her shoulders and flicking the point of her rapier. "So . . . where is he?"

"Josh Brigand?" came a new, higher-pitched voice. "You thought *we* had him?"

A third FIB rogue emerged from the darkness. He was tall, skinny, and his head looked like it had been squashed by a Rwandan bonobo.

"You kidnapped him from in front of Bay City Cinema last night," I said. "We were there."

Both men stared at us blankly, then looked at each other.

"We *just* heard him!" Jeeves said. "We heard Dirk Grimple say he wanted to 'get rid of this scurvy dog . . .'"

He trailed off at the sound of a soft whimper coming from the floor. It was the same sound we'd heard trickling through the vent a few minutes earlier.

Something started to bounce under Grimple's heavy coat, as if his heart was beating out of his chest. Then, a baby fennec fox wrestled clear of the fabric and balanced on wobbly legs atop the unconscious FIB scalawag.

Julianne reached down and picked up the tiny fox by the scruff of his neck. His paws bicycled in the air and he mewled softly.

"Interesting," I said. "I guess whining fennec foxes sound a lot like terrified movie stars with very white teeth."

"Don't hurt him!" the man in the stocking cap yelled across the room. "That's my—"

"*Our* pet!" the second man said. "We have been taking the best care of him! Named him and everything."

The villain's lower lip trembled. It was plain to see that both rogues had a soft spot for the animal.

"If you don't have Josh Brigand," Jeeves said, "then where is he?"

The men didn't answer. They were still staring at the fox in Julianne's hand. Jeeves stepped forward and swung his mallet until it whistled.

"Now listen you two," he said in the same voice he used when I wove all his shoelaces into a bullwhip, "we want to know where Josh Brigand is, or—"

"*Not Sir Soft Ears!*" both men wailed together.

Julianne rolled her eyes. "That's what you call the fox?"

The duo nodded.

"Might I remind you," Jeeves said, "that we also have two swords dangerously close to Deadly Dirk Grimple."

Julianne and I both pointed our swords at the unconscious rogue.

"Right," the first man said, sounding relieved, "we don't want anything to happen to Dirk, either."

"*For sure* not Sir Soft Ears," the second man added, shuffling his feet a little. "But also not Dirk."

"The Danger Gang doesn't hurt animals," Julianne said, tucking the fox into her jacket so only its giant ears poked out. "It's"—she glanced over at me—"part of the Danger Gang *code.*"

FACT: I was glad to see Julianne adding to our code.

DOUBLE FACT: But her timing might not have been the best.

TRIPLE FACT: Actually, my timing was the worst—because the second I said we wouldn't hurt the fox, the two men's faces changed completely.

There was a long silence in the iceberg as some sort of dastardly understanding passed between the FIB goons. Then the man with the skinny head sneered at us.

"Hear that, Brett? They're not going to hurt our pet."

"That's right, Dave. And I don't think they'd hurt Dirk, either," Brett added.

The two men fanned out to opposite sides of the room. My eyes had finally adjusted to the dim light, and in a far corner I saw a very recognizable stash of treasures. The statue of Anubis, the Sky Disk of Nebra—all the relics stolen from our house were there.

The man called Brett snatched up the Lizard of Ubaid, the first artifact my parents ever bought. He swung it through the air a few times. The other man, Dave, crossed to a second pile and grabbed a stone staff.

"If we *really* want to keep our pet," the squashed-headed rogue said, taking a few practice swings with the staff, "all we have to do is capture the Danger Gang."

31
Sinking Feeling!

The two FIB villains paced toward us, glowering and twirling my parents' relics through the air.

"Do you think we can defeat them?" Jeeves asked under his breath.

"We outnumber them," I said. "*And* we've got swords, because of our very important trip to Death Valley."

"It's a bad idea," Julianne whispered.

The two men stalked closer from either side of the telegraph table.

"Are your sword skills rusty, Sato?" I asked. "Because I think I can take them both if—"

"It's not that," Julianne said. She whipped her sword through the heavy air. "Their weapons are thousands of years old. If we fight, they're going to get ruined."

"Stay back!" I said as the villains paced closer. "Not
another step!"

No sooner had I spoken than Jeeves knelt down and
started rooting through the pockets of Dirk Grimple's coat.
He found a revolver and flicked it open. The bullets made a
cold tinkling sound when they hit the floor, and he dropped
the gun as if it were infected. A few seconds later, he snatched
a crinkled pink piece of paper from one of the scalawag's
pockets.

"These are Grimple's clues," Jeeves said, pocketing the
paper. "I say we get out of here while we can."

Our enemies looked ready to leap into action, but Julianne beat them to it. She spun in circles with her sword
whistling—first feinting toward one man, then another. It was
a complicated display that any member of the Capo Ferro
Fencing Academy would have admired. Both rogues watched
her, jaws hanging wide enough to host a colony of Malaysian
honeybees.

After twirling back into the middle of the room, Julianne
stopped right in front of the shortwave radio and telegraph.
Suddenly her sword started to whistle back and forth as she
cut every single wire to shreds. I saw what she was doing and

lunged for the deflated life raft—poking it full of more holes than a Grecian sea sponge.

"To the ladder, Jeeves!" I called. "Sato successfully sabotaged the scalawags!"

Jeeves was already three rungs up when Deadly Dirk Grimple jerked awake. He jolted upright and his eyes locked with mine.

"Snidewater's archenemy!" he screamed at his men. "Get him!"

Grimple snatched his gun off the floor and started fumbling around for bullets. Julianne kicked them into a corner and followed me to the ladder. We raced up the rungs and dove out of the porthole. Jeeves slammed the iron door shut, and the three of us started cranking it closed.

"To the plane, friends!" I yelled.

We dashed over the top of the fake iceberg toward our seaplane. Dirk Grimple's first shot split the wood just a few feet from me. He was shooting up at us from below!

"To the water!" Julianne screamed.

Clearly things were drastic, since my adventure partner still isn't a big fan of the open ocean.

True! But I'm even less of a fan of bullets being shot at us from inside an iceberg!

The three of us dove into the ocean and started swimming for the plane. Another shot split a board right by the waterline.

I cupped my hands around my mouth. "Sorry, you clod-nosed buffoon, we're swimming to safety!"

"*Ronald!*" Jeeves and Julianne screamed.

FSSSSSSSST!
FSSSSSSSSST!

The next two shots whizzed past me on the left and right, seeming to come up at us from below. We made it to the plane, crawled up onto the floats, and slid into the cockpit.

I settled in behind the controls and flipped on the propeller. I was panting almost too hard to speak.

"Deadly Dirk . . . just shot . . . two holes in the iceberg . . . *below* the water line." I caught my breath and grinned at my friends. "I've . . . got a *sinking feeling* that's not going to work out very well."

Jeeves showed that he appreciated my wordplay with his usual tight grimace, but Julianne couldn't even spare a chuckle. I glanced over and saw her remove the wet, shivering baby fox from inside her sweater.

I cleared my throat. "Sato, I have *a sinking feeling* that—"

"It was hysterical," my adventure partner said, craning her neck out of the plane's passenger window to look behind us. "But those three goons are coming fast, so maybe let's laugh about it later!"

Dirk Grimple and his friends had made it out of the porthole just as the seaplane picked up speed. Luckily, it's hard to shoot at a moving plane from the tip of a sinking iceberg.

We headed back toward Capstone Island, flying above a thin layer of gathering fog.

"I *knew* it!" Jeeves said, smacking the dashboard. "The

FIB is trying to take over the whole Liars' Club! That's the master plan!"

I banked the plane around the head of the island and the theater came into view.

"Nice work, Jeeves," Julianne said. "And there's something else . . ."

We both looked at her. The wet, trembling fox tottered on her lap, nibbling her fingers. Julianne took out her adventure journal and started flipping the pages with her free hand.

"That name that Grimple said, *Snidewater*. That has to be the leader of the FIB, right? *That's* who has Josh."

I reached for my own adventure journal but knew there was nothing about Snidewater inside. I couldn't remember ever hearing the name.

"Snidewater," I said. "Jeeves, have you heard tell of him?"

He shook his head. "We could radio Elexander."

"I'll tell you who *definitely* knows about Snidewater," Julianne said, flicking a page of her notebook. "Vivienne DuVoe."

My mind raced to decipher what Julianne was talking about. Ever since we'd left Death Valley, the other members of the Danger Gang had been unwinding mysteries left and right. I was overdue for a dazzling deduction.

Julianne shed her wet sweater and picked up a rag from the floor to wipe off the soaked fox. "Vivienne DuVoe called the man who ordered her to capture us 'Kindfire,' right?"

"Yes," Jeeves said.

"Well, to act 'snide' is the opposite of being 'kind.' And 'water' is the opposite of 'fire.' So 'Snidewater' and 'Kindfire' are opposites. I'd bet they're the same person. That's our mystery villain."

"Brilliant!" Jeeves cheered. "It makes perfect sense."

"But where *is* the FIB?" Julianne wondered. "We still don't know that part."

Jeeves knelt behind the crate. He delicately opened up the wet paper with Dirk Grimple's clues and flattened it across a few slats of wood. Julianne and I turned in our seats to look.

CLUE 1, DELIVER AT 8 P.M.: MEET FIB IN DEEP DARK NIGHT

CLUE 2, DELIVER AT 4 A.M.: IN SMOKY DEN NO STARS FOR LIGHT

CLUE 3, DELIVER AT NOON: SEA US THIS EVE TO ATTEND OUR FEAST

CLUE 4, DELIVER AT 8 P.M.: TREATS FOR ALL WHO BRAVE THE BEAST

Jeeves read it aloud three times. "Sounds like nonsense."

Julianne rubbed the tip of her nose. "Deep dark . . .

smoky den . . . feast . . . That could point to something underground."

"The tunnels?" Jeeves wondered. "If Kindfire and Snidewater are the same person, that means the FIB *owns* Capstone Island. Because Vivienne called Kindfire the owner . . ."

"Maybe the FIB has been there all along," Julianne added. "The smoky den could be the tunnels."

My brain was racing to unwind the clues. I repeated them over and over in my head.

It must be someplace where the stars are blocked out. Blocked out by smoke? Or . . . fog? Fog is smoky . . .

> FACT: That's when it hit me. My most brilliant hunch ever. Enough to make Death Valley a distant memory.

I tried to hold back. I wanted to soak in the feeling.

"There could be another level to the tunnels or . . ." Jeeves trailed off. "Ronald, why are you grinning like that?"

I banked to the right and pretended to peer at the dials on the control panel. The seaplane wobbled a little as I angled the nose up.

"What?" I asked, biting the inside of my cheek to keep from smiling. "I'm not—"

"To use your words," Jeeves said, "you're grinning like a gassy mongoose."

I gave up trying to hide it and beamed from ear to ear.

Julianne rolled her eyes. "Tell us or I'm parachuting out of here."

I cleared my throat. "The fools give it away in the first line. 'Smoky den'. . . . 'no stars for light.' What's something like smoke?"

My friends only gave me blank stares.

"Fog," I said. "Otherwise known as *mist*!"

"Oh, Ronald," Jeeves said. "Are you back on the—"

"Yes!" I interrupted. My nerves were jumping now. "The FIB is in a ship—look, they wrote 'sea us' instead of 'see us'! A ship that only comes out under the cover of fog, with the stars blacked out. A ship people *think* is actually a 'beast,' like it says in the last line of the clue!"

"*Beast*?" Jeeves said, peering at the clue again.

"Friends," I announced, "I have deduced that the FIB is hiding inside the Serpent of the Mist!"

I smiled at Julianne and Jeeves triumphantly, waiting for their astonished gasps. My deduction had come at a crucial moment, and it felt spectacular. I couldn't wait to tell my parents.

Jeeves scowled. "Ronald, this sounds a little like your ideas about Death Valley."

"It's not!" I said. "I'm right this time. I know it."

"I understand about the see-sea mistake, and the talk of a beast," Jeeves said, "but it feels . . . *thin*."

I glowered at him. "Jeeves, you always trust Julianne's deductions, why not mine?"

The butler didn't answer. Julianne reached over and grabbed the clue to study it. After a second I saw her eyes widen. My whole body tightened. My throat went dry.

Was my partner in dazzling schemes about to steal my moment? Was she going to reveal that the *real* answer was hiding right under our noses? She passed the clue over to Jeeves and pointed something out to him.

"Oh," Jeeves muttered. "Ronald, I'm afraid—"

"That Julianne figured it out?" I snapped. "Of course she did! *She's* the clever one!"

I couldn't look at either of them. All the excitement of my deduction was gone. I was sweating and my eyes stung.

Jeeves cleared his throat. "I was going to say, Ronald, I'm afraid I owe you an apology. You're right. The FIB is hiding in the Serpent of the Mist."

I looked away from the controls to face him. "You . . . agree with me?"

Jeeves nodded. "Yes."

"You said the Serpent was important from the beginning," Julianne said. "Very impressive."

"What made you change your—"

Jeeves held the clue under my nose and ran a long, slender finger down the page, pointing at the first letter of each line.

CLUE 1, DELIVER AT 8 P.M.: MEET FIB IN DEEP DARK NIGHT

CLUE 2, DELIVER AT 4 A.M.: IN SMOKY DEN NO STARS FOR LIGHT

CLUE 3, DELIVER AT NOON: SEA US THIS EVE TO ATTEND OUR FEAST

CLUE 4, DELIVER AT 8 P.M.: TREATS FOR ALL WHO BRAVE THE BEAST

"I said it!" I yelled. "You both heard me! Right?"

Jeeves patted me on the shoulder. Julianne gave me a bold wink. It was a perfect moment. Or *almost* perfect. It would have been better if the engine hadn't started to choke and the propellers hadn't fluttered to a stop.

In fact, that would have been a lot better.

The plane burped a few times and went still. It was deadly quiet in the cockpit. We were officially out of gas. There wasn't much danger, of course. We were over the ocean and the theater was in sight. We'd be able to glide all the way there.

Ronald shifted in his seat, awkwardly. "Well . . . we could never have approached the Serpent of the Mist by plane anyway. They would have spotted us."

"It's almost a blessing that we wasted all that gas going to Death Valley," Jeeves teased.

"That's not what I meant," Ronald said, looking sullen.

The plane was losing altitude, but we were closing in on the theater.

"Okay, I admit it," Ronald added after a long silence. "Death Valley wasn't my best idea."

Jeeves grinned at him, then started to chuckle a little. I joined in. After everything we'd been through laughing felt nice. Even Ronald managed to smile.

"What's done is done," Jeeves said.

"And we got swords," I said, giving him a wink.

It was actually kind of peaceful up there without the droning hum of the propellers. We knew where the FIB was hiding now. We knew what they wanted (all of us, captured). We knew they had Josh Brigand.

Soon we'd be in grave peril again. Soon we'd come "face-to-face with evil and villainy," to use Ronald's words. But for a few minutes we were just three friends, drifting above the clouds, soaring silently through an ever-darkening night.

32

Stories by the Fire!

We made it all the way to the harbor before skimming the water. For once the landing really *was* as soft as the belly of a Mexican walking fish. It was quiet too, with the engines completely dead.

Elias and Suraya peeked their heads out the door the moment they heard our voices. They whisked us inside, led us up to their apartment above the theater, and sat us down by the fire. Suraya bustled around the kitchenette for just a second, then brought over three bowls of couscous.

"By any chance did my parents—" I began between bites.

"They were here!" Elias said. "Now they're—"

He stopped when Julianne pulled the napping fennec fox out of her sweater and set it on the rug. Suraya looked at it warily for just a second, then rushed to warm up a saucer of milk for the tiny beast.

"They intercepted a radio message," she said.

"Then rushed off to try to rescue you at the docks," Elias added, ". . . but you're here."

"We tried to radio you from the plane," I said.

"We were down in the tunnels," Elias told me.

There was no time to explain everything we'd uncovered, so we skipped to the most important part.

"We know the secret of the FIB hideout," Julianne said, her eyes wide and bright. "It's a boat called the—"

"Serpent of the Mist," everyone in the room said at once.

The tiny fennec fox ran circles around Julianne's chair, yapping and nipping at her ankles.

"How did you find that out?" I asked.

Suraya shrugged. "Your parents ambushed a group of FIB goons."

"And convinced them to spill their secrets," Elias said. "Mrs. Zupan said, 'Nothing makes a rogue lose his mettle, like threatening to clobber him with a piece of metal.'"

"That certainly sounds like her," Jeeves noted. "But where *is* the Serpent?"

Suraya dropped another log on the fire. "That we don't know. But we do know *what* it is."

"What?" Julianne asked.

Elias's eyes seemed to glow in the firelight. "An illegal gambling ship."

"It comes once or twice a month and stays way off shore," Suraya said. "People hear about it, and they get dropped off in boats, but they never know that it's owned by the FIB. They also don't realize that all the games are rigged for them to lose."

Jeeves snapped his fingers. "Remember? Dirk Grimple said that the headquarters was 'open for business tonight.' That must mean there are people gambling on it."

Julianne sprang to her feet and started pacing. "So let me get this straight. The Serpent of the Mist is a big ship?"

"Yes," Suraya said.

"Where people go to gamble on foggy nights?"

"Exactly."

"But also home to the FIB?"

"Which," I added, standing up to do a little pacing of my own, "is led by a man named Snidewater, who also owns this island, using the name Kindfire."

"And he's the one who has Josh Brigand," Julianne said, clucking her tongue a few times.

"Indeed," Jeeves said. He stood up and started to pace too. It felt familiar somehow, the three of us all pacing through a room like this.

"So all we have to do is sneak aboard this ship," Jeeves went on, "find Snidewater, and rescue Brigand?"

Julianne cast a shadowy glace at him. "Without getting crushed, maimed, or captured."

Jeeves let out a long breath. "Impossible. Can't be done."

Suraya and Elias looked surprised.

"Fear not," I told them. "That's just my dear butler's way of saying 'I'm excited for the next stage of—'"

"No, Ronald, it's not," Jeeves said, looking troubled. "They have a whole crew of FIB; there's three of us."

"Ronald's parents are headed to the boat too," Elias said, "and Julianne's grandfather."

Jeeves didn't look convinced. Julianne eyed me, biting her pinkie nail. "How are the Zupans planning to get on the ship in the first place?"

Finally, a question with an easy answer.

"They'll use disguises," I said. "They always say master adventurers should use disguises whenever possible."

"Exactly," Elias agreed. "We showed them the old movie costumes, down in the tunnels, and when they left Capstone Island, we hardly recognized them."

It was finally out in the open: the FIB had tried to kidnap Jeeves and lure us all to their ship so that they could take over the Liars' Club 'in dramatic fashion.' It was all one big complicated trap. And even Francisco Zupan says that "Traps should be avoided, just like Bolivian wolf scorpions." But what choice did we have? We *had* to go to the Serpent.

That is, *if* we could find it in the first place.

"Suraya, when is Delenda coming to pick you up?" Jeeves asked.

He stood up from his wingback chair and crossed the room to the radio.

"She should be here any minute," the scientist said.

The good butler picked up the receiver and started spinning the dials. "Delenda . . . come in. Delenda?"

This went on for a few minutes of dry crackling and buzzing before a warm voice came to life on the airwaves.

"Tom?" The crabbing boat captain sounded more than a little excited to hear Jeeves's voice. "I've been wondering about you. When are we going to have another game of chess?"

FACT: Even in the firelight, I could see the blood rise in Jeeves's cheeks.

"Soon, I hope," he said. "But I'm afraid before I can take you up on that, I need a . . . favor."

"What's that now?" Delenda asked, her voice turning gruff again.

"Well," Jeeves said, "it so happens that the Serpent of the Mist is a real thing . . . though it's not a serpent. It's a gambling boat, and we have reason to believe that our friend is being held hostage on board. We need help to locate where it is."

Over the radio waves, we heard Delenda set her receiver down. She came back on a few seconds later.

"The men say it's not foggy enough for the Serpent of the Mist to appear," Delenda said.

Jeeves pressed the button on the receiver. "I have a . . . a *hunch* that it will come out tonight. Would you keep your eyes peeled?"

"I think I told you that I don't do favors," Delenda said. There was a long pause before the crabbing captain's voice crackled to life again. "I'll put a call out. If the Serpent is near Bay City, *someone* will spot it."

Jeeves gave another one of his famous sighs, but this one was full of relief. "Thank you."

He clicked off the line. I looked down at my clothes from the movie premiere. They were wet, torn, and stained with sweat.

"If Delenda finds the Serpent, we'll need disguises," I said. "Clothes, hats . . . some sort of facial hair."

Without any more explanation, Elias jumped to his feet and led the way through the theater, then down into the boiler room. We ran as a group through the main tunnel until we came to a mint-green door with a pebbled glass window. I hadn't noticed it the night before, but the word COSTUMES was stenciled there in white paint.

"There's a makeup room a few doors down," Elias said.

"Do they have fake mustaches?" I asked.

"I'll check!"

He ducked down the hall, and Jeeves, Julianne, and I stepped inside the costume room. It was huge—with giant, rolling clothes racks creating a strange sort of maze. There was a whole section of old armor and a row of glossy pink leotards.

We split up to walk along the aisles. We couldn't see one another, but the sound carried.

"We need a story," I said, sorting through the clothes and looking for pieces that might fit me. "Something that makes sense for why we'd be showing up on this boat."

I could hear Julianne take a hanger off the rack a few rows away. "And we have to look different too," she said. "They're expecting a tall British butler and two kids."

"Yet another problem," Jeeves said from somewhere off to my right. "It's not exactly easy to make children look like adults."

I grabbed a light tan shirt and a pair of green pants. Then added a felt fedora and a pair of boots. I also grabbed a tan bomber jacket. I could hear my friends snatching things off the racks too.

It was hard to really think about how to fool the FIB, but I'd been cold for two days straight except for our time in the desert, so I decided I'd at least get clothes that might warm me up. I chose a sequined green dress, a heavy mink coat, and a headpiece with all sorts of fake jewels on it. I also got some long canary-yellow gloves.

I was just bundling everything together when I reached the middle of the clothes maze and bumped right into Jeeves. He was already changed, wearing a red British officer's jacket that was covered with sashes and medals. His pants were black, with a red stripe down the side, and he had a monocle in one eye.

When he saw me, he stopped to survey his whole outfit. For a second, he looked like he might be sick.

"I don't know what I was thinking," he said. "So silly. This outfit feels absolutely—"

"Dashing!" Ronald called, as soon as he spotted his butler. "You can tell them that you're some sort of British officer, and Julianne and I are your old friends from Bay City."

"But we're *eleven*," I said. "People are going to be able to tell."

That only stumped him for a second. "We'll say we're actors for the Capstone Motion Picture Company! Actors *try* to look young, and they're always shorter than you imagine. Just look at Josh Brigand!"

I was opening my mouth to defend Josh when Elias burst through the door.

"Didn't you guys hear us yelling?" he called across the sea of costumes. "Delenda is here and she's going to take you to the Serpent! Right now!"

33

Fog Rolls In!

"The Serpent of the Mist was spotted by an octopus boat, due west of here," Captain Delenda said as soon as Jeeves, Julianne, and I had jumped onto the deck of her ship. "They said it looked like it was headed south. It shouldn't take more than twenty minutes to catch up."

Delenda motioned for us to follow her into her cabin. Elias and Suraya hung back at the sea wall.

"Aren't you coming?" Julianne called.

"We'll wait here," Suraya said. "Delenda said she'd bring us to the mainland after she drops you off."

"You've been too good to us," I said, winking at Elias. "Next time we meet, we should talk about you becoming a *full* member of the Danger Gang."

A wide smile broke across his face.

Jeeves stepped inside right away, but Julianne and I hung

back. The crabbers must've heard we were headed to the Serpent, because they stared at us like two Tasmanian blobfish.

Inside the cabin, we could hear Jeeves and Delenda chatting. Delenda said something and Jeeves laughed as if it was the funniest thing he'd ever heard. This was strange since he hardly ever laughs at my hysterical jokes.

"Want to go sit up by the bow?" Julianne asked.

"Sure thing, Sato," I said.

We set down the satchel and our costumes by the cabin door and walked toward the front of the ship. There was a giant anchor up there, a few huge piles of rope coiled on the deck, and two old crab traps.

Julianne sat on one trap and I took the other. The bow of the boat dipped and rose with the waves but not enough to bother us. The ocean was blue-black, just like the sky.

"I could use a nap," Julianne said. "For about a week straight."

I smiled at her. "Indeed. This mission has been a dizzying one."

We stared out at the horizon. The fog was beginning to gather—it made your skin feel clammy. The air smelled like rotting seaweed.

Julianne tapped a rope with her toe a few times. I glanced over my shoulder at the window of Delenda's cabin—she and Jeeves were deep in conversation. I decided to get something off my chest.

"Sorry about Death Valley," I said.

Julianne looked at me for a long minute and lifted one shoulder. "Why did you do it?"

I picked at a barnacle stuck to the trap I was sitting on. "I swear it made sense at the time."

"Yeah?" my adventure partner seemed suspicious.

"I mean . . . it made less sense once you woke up." I flicked the barnacle overboard. "Also, I guess I was hoping to see my parents . . . I wanted their help."

Julianne gazed out over the water. The fog was turning

into a thick soup. "Well . . . that's better than it being just because you were worried about the second-adventure slu—"

"It was that too," I admitted.

Julianne drew her sword from its sheath, held out the blade, and looked down the line. "Well, no chance for a slump now, right?"

"Let's just get Brigand home safe," I told her. "I know you two are dear friends."

Julianne tilted her head and thought about it. "I guess we are. I mean you have your parents and Jeeves. I just have my grandfather. It gets lonely. And Josh is so nice to me."

I nodded.

"You still hate him, though, don't you?" she asked.

I looked down at my lap and shook my head. "I don't hate him. I just get sort of . . . *jealous* of him."

I picked off another barnacle and dropped it next to my feet.

"Because he's famous and rich?" Julianne asked.

I started picking at the crab trap again. "Just . . . everything. You always say how he's so great."

Julianne gave a tiny shrug. "I mean . . . I say nice things about you, too."

I looked over at her. "You do?"

Our eyes met. "Mostly when you're not around."

A long pause passed between us. I broke off a third

barnacle, then a fourth. If this conversation lasted much longer, the crab trap I was sitting on would look like new.

"Is it bad?" I finally asked. "Wanting everyone to think I'm great?"

Julianne took her time to think about it as the ship motored on into the dark night. "I mean . . . I get it. I was so good on the first adventure. Then on this one I was wrong about some things. I never thought for a second that the Serpent of the Mist was real. And it made me wonder, 'What if I'm never quite as good again?'"

The fog had swallowed us now. Her head looked like it was floating, like some sort of ghost.

"That's exactly it," I said. "After the first adventure I thought everything would change, but it wasn't any different."

Julianne smiled. "I know."

I picked another barnacle off the trap. "Instead of becoming internationally famous, I have to go to public school."

"It's not *that* bad."

We were interrupted by a voice cutting through the thickening fog.

"Let me tell you two a story," Jeeves said.

He strode toward us and set a hand on the rail of the crabbing boat. With his fancy uniform, he made a pretty striking figure. His medals jangled with each step.

"When I was a young man, I won the highest honor

in the Butlering League of England: Royal Ganymede Society."

"BLERGS?" Julianne asked.

"It was a bad acronym," Jeeves said, leaning against the rail. "Anyway, after winning, I started traveling the world with Francisco. In Moldova, we came upon a similar butlering contest."

Julianne and I traded looks.

"I came in third," Jeeves went on, looking over our heads at the cabin of the ship. "And I had to learn: no matter how good you are, someone out there might be better."

I glanced over at my partner in grand adventures. "This is a real pick-me-up, hey Sato?"

Julianne smirked. "A definite morale booster."

Jeeves plowed on. "The next year, I practiced nonstop. I went back to Moldova and entered the contest again." He wet his lips and smirked.

"And?" Julianne asked.

"I got fourth."

I threw another barnacle overboard into the darkness. The fog was so thick now, you could practically chew it.

"Even when you work hard, sometimes, you're going to struggle," Jeeves said. "No matter how much effort you give. Sometimes things just won't work out. That's why you need people to help you when things aren't going well." He stood tall, straightening the cuffs of his officer's jacket, and winked at Delenda. I could see a thought dawning across Julianne's face.

"Oh my gosh, Jeeves," Julianne said, "did you come up here to give us that speech while looking handsome in your disguise, just so Delenda would notice?"

Jeeves gazed out at the ocean again. "I found the story fitting," he mumbled.

"Yeah, *right*!" Julianne said. "You were trying to be impressive!"

We both started to laugh while Jeeves toyed with one of the medals on his coat. "I suppose . . ."

"Well if *that's* your goal," Julianne said, popping to her feet.

I charged over to Jeeves, talking loud enough so Delenda could hear through the window. "Jeeves, you are so wise! What amazing advice you just gave us! We feel much better now!"

Then I wrapped him up in a huge hug. Side note: even though I was trying to help him look impressive, it was really nice to get a hug. It'd been a long two days. As we hugged, I angled my face to look at Delenda. I could just barely see her through the fog. She was watching us and smiling, with her head sort of tilted to the side.

"This is totally working," I muttered to Jeeves.

"I owe you one," he said under his breath.

As quickly as it had arrived, Delenda's smile froze, then vanished. I let go of Jeeves and turned to face forward again.

Out ahead of us was a cloud of fog. Inside the cloud, red and blue sparks spouted into the sky.

FACT: We'd found the Serpent of the Mist.

34

Sea and Enemies!

We watched a fountain of sparks soar into the sky and scatter. A minute later, we could hear what the crabbers had called the "cries of anguished souls" drifting across the water.

"It's just laughing and yelling," Julianne said, "the way adults always do at parties."

She was right. The chorus of tipsy screams and braying laughter sounded like some sort of monster from far away, but it clearly wasn't. As Delenda eased off the throttle, we could even make out tiny snatches of conversation.

"Has anyone seen my *purse*? I put it down right here!"

"My, it *does* get hot in there, hey gents?"

"Where *is* everyone getting the cotton candy! Charla! *Chaaar-laaa!* Get me some cotton candy, won't you?"

There was a knock on the glass window of the cabin and Delenda motioned us to come inside. We walked around the bow to the other side of the cabin and Julianne stooped down to grab our bundled-up disguises.

"Listen," Delenda said the second we were inside, "my crew does not want to tangle with the Serpent."

"But the Serpent of the Mist is just a ship," Julianne said. "They can see it, right there."

The captain didn't blink. "Did you ever think that maybe whoever's aboard is just as dangerous as a sea monster?"

It was a fair point. I felt my heart speed up.

"Now, you can't swim over there," Delenda said, "so we're giving you our life boat."

Jeeves stepped forward. "Delenda, we can't let you do that. What if something happens?"

Delenda straightened up. She was every inch as tall as the good butler. "Tom, I am Captain Delenda Jean-Baptiste, and I know every rock and current in these waters. Don't you *dare* worry about me."

Jeeves looked like an abandoned elephant for just a second, when Delenda leaned forward. "We'll *both* be careful, agreed?"

I ducked behind a curtain that sectioned off Delenda's closet from the rest of the room and changed into my disguise.

The mink coat dragged on the ground a little, but everything else fit okay.

Delenda smiled at me. "You look lovely, sweetheart."

"Indeed," Ronald said.

We all faced him, and his eyes widened.

"I . . . I just mean . . . ," he stammered, "it's an . . . adventurous disguise, is what I'm saying. Bold. Daring."

Delenda led Jeeves and me back on deck, while Ronald stayed to change into his disguise in the privacy of the cabin. The crew of the crabbing boat had the bright orange raft inflated and waiting in the water. Its outboard motor puttered away.

Ronald came out of Delenda's cabin dressed in green pants and a light tan shirt. He wore a brown bomber jacket and a felt fedora.

"That's your disguise?" Jeeves asked.

"I don't have my mustache glued on yet," Ronald said.

"That's *literally* an outfit you already own."

"Yeah," I said, "I think that's exactly what you wore over to my house last Wednesday."

Ronald scowled. "We'll tell them I'm a movie star. I've been called in to play the sorts of adventurous roles Josh Brigand landed before his mysterious disappearance."

It wasn't going to fool anyone, but there wasn't much we could do about it. We climbed into the life raft and waved to the crabbers. Jeeves sat at the back to steer, and we motored toward the Serpent of the Mist—just as another wild explosion of sparks sprayed from one of its smokestacks.

The water lapped against the side of the raft as we buzzed toward our enemies' lair. Jeeves steered and Julianne helped me glue the pencil-thin mustache that Elias had found to my upper lip.

"So, you're a British general," Julianne said to Jeeves, "and Ronald and I are friends of yours in the movie business. Ronald is an actor, and I'm a writer."

We could see the hulking shape of the boat now, out in front of us. It had a paddle wheel at the back and two huge smokestacks in the middle. The sparks leaped out of the tops of the stacks, and when the breeze caught them, they *did* look like the fiery breath of a sea monster.

Each time a new blast of sparks exploded into the sky, we heard the revelers cheer and scream.

"Wait," Julianne said. "Ronald and I shouldn't have swords if we're in the movie business. Jeeves, you strap them to your waist and stay between us. If we need them, we can draw them from there."

"I'll take the satchel," I told my friends, stuffing Jeeves's polo mallet into the bag. "It fits with my disguise."

We neared the ship, but there didn't seem to be anywhere to climb aboard. The rails were all ten feet off the water. I was just opening my mouth to say something, when a man waved a lantern at us from near the bow and motioned for Jeeves to drive around to the other side. We rounded the front of the ship and saw two men in white tuxedo jackets guarding a floating gangplank where a dozen other boats were tied up.

Jeeves nosed in next to a sleek, fancy speedboat, and I tied us to the makeshift dock. The two men waited at a break in the railing, where the plank met the boat. They both had bulges under their arms. The sort of bulges that FIB members have when there's a gun holster hiding beneath a poorly fitted jacket.

"Look," Julianne said under her breath. "Out there."

She motioned with her head and I saw it: a small sailboat with one person aboard, cutting through the fog under the light of the crescent moon.

"The woman in the cape?" I asked.

Julianne squinted into the distance. "It's certainly possible."

"Well let's hope that she's not an enemy," Jeeves said with a nervous glance at the FIB guards. "We have enough of those as it is."

We walked up the gangplank together.

"Stop, you three," one of the men said, holding out a hand. His voice was like the snarl of a Siberian wolf. "Give us the password."

The three of us froze. My compatriots looked to me for an answer.

"That's a trick question," I said after a long pause. "There *is* no password."

The man who asked the question scowled and looked at his partner. He started to reach into his jacket. I could see the pistol in a holster under his armpit.

"Just joking old chap!" Jeeves said, patting the guard on the shoulder. "It's 'Mist.' The password is 'Mist.'"

Without another word, the two men stepped aside. Julianne, Jeeves, and I slipped past them in silence. When we were five steps away, Julianne let out a huge breath.

"Nice thinking, Jeeves," she said.

"It was luck," the good butler replied. "And I'm afraid we'll need a lot more of it."

The far side of the ship had fewer people, but we could hear the crowds up at the bow, screaming as another spray of sparks exploded skyward. We walked along the railing until we came to a sliding door with wide smoked-glass windows

that you couldn't quite see through. Inside, we heard the blare of a brass band.

I grabbed the door and slid it open. "Once again, friends, we venture inside the belly of the beast."

35

A Party for the Ages!

A tidal wave of noise crashed over us the second we stepped inside the Serpent of the Mist. It was a roaring party, loaded with people spinning in all directions. The smell of firecracker smoke wafted across the room, and you couldn't go two seconds without hearing a champagne cork pop or glasses clinking together.

There were at least fifteen musicians and five singers crowded onto the stage. Anyone not busy with instruments danced with their hands high, elbowing for a corner of the spotlight.

Jeeves ducked low so that his mouth was near our ear level. "Where will we find Josh Brigand or Snidewater in this sea of people? We don't even know what Snidewater looks like."

It was another tough question. Ten men in three-piece suits brushed past us, and I could easily imagine any of them being the FIB chief. How were we supposed to tell?

"This one's a slow song!" the bandleader announced into his microphone.

A chorus of "no's" went up from the crowd. They stomped and whistled until the band gave up and played more dancing music. Women in shimmery dresses twirled across the hardwood floor, followed by men in tuxedos.

A hundred blue balloons fell from the rafters. I looked up and spotted more men in suits, dumping them from the catwalks. As soon as the balloons settled, they started pouring out buckets of confetti.

"I'll give the FIB this much," I said to my friends, "they know how to throw a party."

"This boat definitely seems like a better hideout than Zeetan Z's cave back in Borneo," Julianne agreed.

It also smelled better. A *lot* better.

Above the dance floor, a huge crystal chandelier caught the light and reflected tiny diamond-shaped rainbows across the walls. A few of the balloons were bounced into the air by partygoers, grazed the chandelier, and popped.

Jeeves put his hand out and stopped a waiter who was ferrying a tray of champagne coupes across the room.

"Excuse me, old chap," he said. "I'm an old chum of the owner of this boat. Do you know where I could find him?"

The waiter stopped and looked us up and down. "Who?"

"The . . . boss?" Jeeves said. "*Snidewater?*"

The tray of champagne glasses rattled a little. The waiter couldn't have been more than seventeen years old, and his uniform was three sizes too big.

He bit his lip and took a quick look around the room. Then he leaned close to us. "I've never seen him myself, at least not that I can be sure of. He's very private . . ." He paused. "I *hear* he stays near the Scorpion Poker table."

Jeeves tipped his hat and headed in toward the gambling pit, weaving past a fire twirler standing on one pedestal and a sword swallower perched a few feet away. A man wearing a bright yellow suit hopped up on a cocktail table. He was holding a box full of bottle rockets and Roman candles.

"We're lighting fireworks at midnight!" he announced, almost slipping off the table.

A whole crowd of people pushed toward him, spilling drinks and elbowing one another.

"Oh darling, don't you simply love these parties," a woman gushed to no one in particular, stepping on my adventure partner's coat. "They really are *divine.*"

Julianne rolled her eyes.

At the edge of the gambling pit, Jeeves stopped again. He'd snatched a drink off a tray somewhere along the way, and held it in front of his mouth so that no dastardly FIB member could read his lips.

"Right-o then, friends," he said, "what's the plan?"

I pretended I was about to sneeze, so that no one could see my mouth move either. "Well, Snidewater is probably the only one who knows where Brigand is. We either find him or have to search the ship."

Julianne faked a yawn so that she had a good reason to hide her mouth too. "It's a *huge* ship. But we've also never seen Snidewater in our lives."

"The waiter said he stays near the Scorpion Poker table," I said, faking a second sneeze. "That's a start."

Julianne pretended to yawn again. "Ronald, your family plays that game, right?"

"Indeed," I said. "It's the game of kings and queens—the most difficult game on earth. It's full of bluffing, feints, and trickery. A game . . ."

I trailed off, distracted by just how high Jeeves's left eyebrow was traveling up his forehead. He looked over the rim of his glass at Julianne. "It's a silly game, really. Simple too."

"Well," Julianne said through her third fake yawn, "maybe if we go over there and play, we can figure out who Snidewater is. But you'll have to teach me how to play."

I was going to have to fake a lot of sneezes to teach her what she needed to know about the brilliant game of Scorpion Poker. Instead, I reached for my adventure journal, flipped to the page where I'd written the rules down, and held it out.

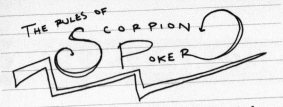

THE RULES OF SCORPION POKER

1. The "Scorpion deck" uses any eighteen cards from a regular deck, plus two jokers—making twenty cards total.
2. The jokers are "the scorpions," and they're the only cards that matter.
3. Each hand, everyone is dealt one card. From there, the game is all about bluffing.
4. Everyone has to raise the bet or fold. The betting doesn't stop until there are only two people left.
5. Right before the cards are flipped, either of the last two players can fold. If they do, they only lose half their chips.
6. If neither one folds, the cards are flipped. Only a player with a scorpion can win the pot. If neither person has a scorpion, they split it. They also split it if both people have a scorpion.
7. No one can quit the game until they're completely out of chips.

"Got it," Julianne said after about twelve seconds. She snapped the journal shut and passed it back to me.

"Don't you want a few more minutes?" I asked. "Do you need me to tell you about the—"

"It's literally the easiest game ever. Let's go."

She cut a path toward the gambling pit. The carpet was thick and deep red. The tables were draped in red velvet. In the corner sat a table shaped like a half-moon. Beside it was a sign that read:

SCORPION POKER

The table was ringed by six men standing shoulder to shoulder. They were big shoulders too, the sort that make the seams of a suit jacket look ready to pop.

> **FACT:** Any one of the six could have been the dastardly villain we were hunting for.

One man had a scar on his cheek, another had a jaw that looked like it could chew bolts, and a third had sunken eyes ringed with baggy skin. Julianne, Jeeves, and I found the last three seats at the table. Jeeves sat at one end, I sat at the other, and Julianne found a spot in the middle of the six burly men.

The dealer had slicked-back blond hair, a narrow face, and watery blue eyes. He pushed stacks of chips toward Jeeves, Julianne, and me. Jeeves reached for his wallet but the dealer waved him off.

"We play on the honor system," he said with a broad grin. "I'm sure you'll pay up soon enough."

The dealer shuffled the deck, making the cards snap together crisply while the six men stared us down like angry water buffaloes.

"Cards coming out," the dealer chirped. "Beware the scorpion's sting!"

36

The Scorpion's Sting!

As the dealer slid a card to each of us across the felt table, I studied the six brawny men. Would Snidewater be the one with the scar on his face? The one with the sunken eyes? The one with the bulging jaw?

I figured I could rule out the man with a stain on his suit coat. The villain we were looking for seemed too precise for that. Another one of the men had a strange haircut that made his ears look too big for his head. I had a feeling Snidewater wasn't that one either . . . but the FIB isn't exactly known for good grooming.

Then again, maybe the villain wasn't at the table at all. Maybe he was watching from up in the rafters or playing roulette. Maybe he was the band leader.

"The betting is to you," the dealer said.

I snapped back to attention and looked at my card for the first time. It wasn't a joker. I glanced around and saw Jeeves fiddling with one of the buttons of his coat.

Without wasting a second, I tossed my card back toward the dealer. Around the Zupan home, it's well known that if Jeeves starts fidgeting with some bit of clothing, he has a good card. Two of the men folded next and so did Julianne. Two of the other men hung around to bet a few times, then threw their cards away too.

Finally, it was just Jeeves and the man with the scar on his cheek. The man with the scar bet everything. Jeeves hesitated, then did the same. Neither of them folded during the final round of betting.

The dealer motioned to the man with the scar and he turned over a two of diamonds.

"I was bluffing," he grunted, "but I think you were too."

Jeeves smiled coolly and flipped over a joker. I saw that it was specially designed to actually look like a scorpion.

"Cheerio, old chap," Jeeves said as the man with the scar snorted and shoved away from the table. "Better luck next go."

The dealer riffled the cards. "Nicely done. Who taught you how to play?"

The good butler was still raking in his chips. "I learned from the Zuuuu—"

He caught himself just in time, then snatched a handkerchief from his breast pocket and dabbed his forehead.

The man with the big jaw grunted. "The *zoo?*"

All five of the men still left at the table glared at Jeeves.

"Y-yes quite," he stammered. "The zoo. I used to work there, and the men who clean the python cages absolutely adore this game."

"But you're a general," the man with the sunken eyes grunted. "Why would a general work in a zoo?"

Jeeves swallowed hard. After a long pause, the dealer rescued him.

"Next hand, coming out! Beware the scorpion's sting!"

The game went on like this for twenty minutes or so. The whole time I was looking around the gambling area, hoping to see something that would help us figure out who Snidewater was. I looked for anything suspicious, anyone watching us. I checked out the fire twirler and the sword swallower and every waiter who came within ten feet.

Nothing. I still didn't have any idea about whether or not Snidewater was nearby. It worried me. We couldn't just go on playing cards all night, even though we did seem to be pretty good at the game. By the time we'd played ten hands, five of the men in suits had lost their chips and stepped back from the table. The only one left was the man with bulging jaw muscles.

"A spectacular game," came a voice over my shoulder.

Three chairs jerked out from the table and three fresh players sat down. Two of the new players wore heavy makeup to look old. They walked with hunched backs and wore musty clothing. The man had thick glasses and a white beard. The woman walked with a cane.

None of it mattered. I still recognized them as Francisco and Helen Zupan. The third person in their group didn't need a disguise to look old.

"Hello," the elderly Japanese man said to me as he pulled out his stool.

His eyes were bright and serious. I kept staring but didn't answer. I was too worried I'd accidentally say what was on the tip of my tongue: "Hi, Grandpa."

Jeeves, Julianne, and I did our best to act like we didn't recognize my parents and Mr. Sato sitting down at the table. I'd been starting to worry that we'd never find Snidewater or

rescue Josh Brigand, but seeing my parents in makeup and costumes made me feel as brave as an Ecuadorian sea eagle.

"Next hand coming out," the dealer said.

The betting went quick. My dad bet half his chips right away, and most everyone else dropped out. I looked at my card and slumped my shoulders in disappointment.

> **FACT:** It was all a ploy! I had a joker.

The man with the heavy jaw raised the bet and I raised back. I thought my dad would keep playing, but he tossed his card toward the dealer.

"It's just you and me," the man with the iron jaw said, "and I'm betting everything I've got. Are you *brave* enough for that?"

His chips clicked and tinkled together as he shoved them toward the dealer.

"Indeed," I said, pushing my own stack of chips into the middle.

Staring down this ruffian, I started to feel certain that we'd found Snidewater. He glowered back at me as if he could see right through my disguise. I glanced over at Jeeves, wishing he'd move closer so I could grab my sword from his belt.

We flipped our cards over at the same time.

"Two scorpions!" the pale-eyed dealer cheered. "You split the chips!"

He started counting them out, then paused.

"Of course," the dealer said, "you could always flip a coin to break the tie."

The man with the giant jaw grunted his approval and I was feeling too bold to back down. The dealer drew a gold coin from his pocket. He looked at me. "You call heads or tails."

He flipped the coin up in the air, and it spiraled above us.

"Heads," I said.

The dealer slapped the coin onto the back of his hand and held it toward me. The coin landed on tails, but I hardly even noticed that I'd lost. I was looking at an eagle with its wings spread. An image I'd seen that same morning, in Death Valley, at Neesy's Rare Treasures.

The coin showed the initials "EB" stamped on it, just like the coin in Death Valley. But this time the initials were stamped on the chest. Instantly I knew that I was looking at my parents' missing doubloon.

I looked up at the card dealer. His features were tight and his pale eyes were narrow, sinister. Almost snakelike. Snidewater.

I opened my mouth to yell, but a heavy body tackled me from behind and all the air left my lungs. We crashed into the table and chips spilled everywhere. Strangers dove for them, and complete chaos broke out in the gambling pit.

My friends and parents crashed down beside me, fighting off FIB goons of their own. The villains wrenched our arms behind us until we writhed in pain.

Snidewater took off the clip-on bow tie he'd been wearing and dropped it on the floor. "The Zupans and the Danger Gang in my clutches. My master plan is all coming together."

37

In the Brig with Brigand!

The FIB rogues jerked us to our feet and marched us toward a door at the back of the gambling pit. I tried to squirm free, but there was something metal pressed hard against my spine. It felt like the barrel of a pistol.

Snidewater leaned close to one of his men. "Get everyone who isn't with the FIB off the ship. Tell them that we've caught a gang of thieves, and they need to get back to Bay City."

"You're a scalawag and a villain," I said, glaring at him, "and you'll—"

"Never get away with this?" Snidewater interrupted. "What a wonderful example of irony for me to laugh about while you're rotting in the brig."

"But you *won't* get away with it," Francisco said. "And we will be the ones laughing."

Snidewater froze and held up a hand. His men stopped on a dime. We were at the edge of the gambling pit, right next to the door. The treacherous rogue gazed out over the crowd, his eyes scanning every face. Only a few people were still watching us.

Without warning, Snidewater bent his knees, exploded forward, and drove his fist right into my father's stomach. Francisco gave a groan, and the man holding him let him slip to the carpet.

"*Dad!*" I yelled, fighting to get free as my father gasped for breath.

Snidewater chuckled. "How's that for irony?"

1) Punching Francisco while an FIB stooge held him wasn't ironic, it was just cruel.

2) It made me so mad that I kicked Snidewater in the shins. Which also wasn't ironic but was totally worth it.

Snidewater hopped around for a few minutes after getting kicked, then leaned his face close, until he was practically touching noses with Julianne.

"You're the girl from the radio," he said.

"Julianne Sato," my adventure partner replied. "And I'm not afraid of you."

Snidewater smiled and Julianne's nose wrinkled from his breath.

"Well you should be," the villain hissed. "Because my master plan doesn't end well for you, Julianne Sato."

The FIB shoved us down a dark staircase toward the ship's lower hold. The bottom level of the stern-wheeler was quiet, damp, and smelled like mold. We entered a long room with three solid iron doors lining a wall.

"I don't want them together conspiring," Snidewater said, reaching down to rub his shin. "Two to a cell."

The FIB stooges threw my mother and Mr. Sato through the first door, and my father and Jeeves through the next.

"Boss, there's only one more cell," the man with the stained suit coat said. "And the movie star is in there."

Snidewater looked down at Julianne and me, then gave a shrug. "They're just kids. Throw them in with the dumb actor."

"*His name is Josh Brigand,*" I said, glaring up at the rogue. "And you're a fool for underestimating the Danger Gang."

"We caught you in five minutes, a day ahead of schedule," Snidewater said. "You barely even escaped Vivienne DuVoe on Capstone Island. If anything, we *overestimated* you."

One of the men unlocked the door and slid it open. Sure enough, Brigand was there, sitting on a bunk, glum and haggard. When he saw us, his eyes widened for just a second, then he realized that we'd arrived in the hands of the FIB, and his whole frame sagged.

"Remember when you said that the Danger Gang would rescue you?" Snidewater asked with a sneer. "Well, that worked out about as well as the plot of your last movie."

The FIB toughs snorted their laughter, then shoved Julianne and me inside the cell. Snidewater slammed the iron door.

"Josh!" Julianne said. "Are you—"

She stopped when a slot in the door slid open.

"Sleep tight, friends," Snidewater said. "Don't let the bedbugs bite. And there are *lots* of bedbugs."

"So many," Brigand muttered, scratching a patch of red bites on his wrist.

Julianne tried to make eye contact, but the movie star wouldn't look up. "Josh, I was worried that they'd torture you."

The actor studied the floor. "They did. My movie was reviewed in the paper this morning, and the guard has been taunting me with it all day."

Julianne's forehead wrinkled. "Oh, well that's not as bad as—"

"Did you two think it was full of 'lazy jokes'?" Brigand interrupted.

"Well," I said, "the part with the dung throwing—"

"It's not important," Julianne said. "We need to get out of here. Josh, tell us everything."

Brigand lifted one shoulder, then let it drop again.

"It's just one guard," he said. "Every few hours he opens the slot and teases me while he slurps a cup of coffee."

"What else?" I asked.

The movie star didn't answer.

"Josh," Julianne pressed. "You told me once that good acting was all in the details. Well you're my favorite actor and now we *need* details."

Josh raised his head. "Details, huh?" He let the words soak in, then straightened up a little. "Okay . . . well, halfway through his coffee, the guard sets his cup down on the tray where they're supposed to pass me food. Then he paces the halls reading different lines from the review so that they echo through my cell."

"Oh, Josh," Julianne said, moving toward him and putting a hand on his shoulder. "It *can't* be that bad."

"No? You should hear what the *Bay City Chronicle* said about the main character of my movie. And I don't know if you two noticed, but I based that character off *myself*!"

"We noticed," I said. "We definitely noticed."

Julianne shot me a look. "Go back to the coffee. Where does the guard set it?"

Brigand pointed to the slot in the iron door, which was closed now. "On the other side of that slot there's a flip-up tray. He leaves it there just to taunt me. The smell of coffee only makes me long for the comforts of home and the—"

"He just leaves his coffee there?" Julianne interrupted.

The fluorescent lights flickered overhead.

"Yes," Brigand said. "Why?"

Julianne flashed a broad smile and winked at me. "Friends, I have an incredible idea."

Okay, okay. I know that winking and announcing my idea that way sounded kind of . . . well, kind of like Ronald. But it was a good idea. If he can announce everything that way, I wanted to see if I could pull it off.

FACT: And she definitely did!

38

Escape Plan Brewing!

Julianne paced through our cell, tapping a finger against her pursed lips. Brigand glanced at me, confused, but I motioned for him to wait. As my father always says, "An adventurer should never be interrupted while thinking up a plan. Unless there's a tarantula on her back."

"The coffee is the key here," Julianne finally said, turning on her heel to face us. "Josh, when was the last time the guard opened that slat in the cell door?"

Brigand thought back. "Maybe two hours before you got thrown in here. He's overdue, come to think of it."

Julianne started pacing again. "Well, here's the plan: the next time he puts his coffee down and walks away, we're going to sneak this sleeping serum into his drink."

She held up a skinny glass vial full of slow-moving, silvery liquid. I recognized it right away from Vivienne DuVoe's cupboard.

"Then," Julianne said, looking between Josh and me, "we'll tell the guard we poisoned him and show him the vial. But instead of telling him it's the sleeping serum, we'll say it's the antidote."

"Why would he believe us?" Brigand asked.

"He'll start to feel sleepy," I said, getting excited. "When he feels sleepy, he'll know we weren't lying."

A smirk curled Julianne's lips. "Exactly. He'll open the door. If he falls asleep, great. If not, we'll give him the rest of the vial, pretending it's the antidote."

"*Nicely done*, Sato," I said.

Julianne stopped pacing and we both looked at Josh. His body didn't seem quite as slumped as before.

"It's a start," he admitted. "But how will we get off the ship?"

"Brigand," I said, "in the words of Helen Zupan, 'Wait to make your next plan until you've finished the first one, or the weight of the possibilities will crush you.'"

The actor's brow furrowed.

"He's saying that we'll figure out the next part when we get to it," Julianne said. "For now, we just need to get the serum in the guard's drink."

Brigand rubbed a hand across his stubble. "Oh, he won't notice a thing. He'll be nose deep in reading the horrible reviews for *Buccaneers of the South Seas*."

We sat quietly, waiting for the guard to slide open the slat in the iron door. I kept running through what to do in my head. I'd have to move quickly and make sure that I wasn't seen.

Meanwhile, it seemed like Ronald was finally warming up to Josh. Soon, they were deep in conversation.

"What if my fans completely forget about me just because *Buccaneers of the South Seas* is a failure?" Josh wondered aloud.

"Brigand," Ronald said, "I know how you're feeling. I've been worried that if this mission fails, my career as a master adventurer might never recover."

Josh picked at the cuffs of his tuxedo jacket. "I mean, who am I, really, if I'm not Josh Brigand, beloved actor?"

"And who am I, if I'm not a master adventurer with a dashing mustache?"

"I meant to mention that," Josh said. "It's a nice touch."

While they talked, I stood with my back pressed against the cool iron door, looking down at the vial. I didn't know how much of the serum Vivienne had put in our tea. I didn't want to give the guard too little to affect him—I'd only get one chance. Still, it would be nice to save some, in case we needed it again.

"I guess the key is just to try harder than ever to impress my fans," Josh said.

The words caught my attention. Ronald nodded along, as if this was some piece of incredible wisdom.

"Yes, exactly," he said. "We should always be impressive."

It hurt my head to listen to them.

"You two literally couldn't be more wrong," I said.

They stared at me, confused.

"The last thing either of you needs is to try harder to impress people," I said.

"So . . . ," Josh said after a long pause, "who should we try to impress?"

"Just be yourselves!"

Ronald nodded thoughtfully. "I think Sato means that we should try to be impressive but *tell* everyone that we aren't trying at all. You know, by saying things like, 'It's hardly a challenge for a master adventurer like me!' and 'I make bravery look easy!'"

Brigand's eyes lit up. "Got it! I could say things like, 'Yes, I am very handsome, but I hardly noticed because I'm the most humble man alive.'" He turned to me. "How did that sound?"

I looked down at the vial, wondering if there was enough sleeping potion to knock the two of them out for a few minutes.

"What I'm saying is that you should both just be yourselves," I said.

They looked sheepish, and I was sure that my words had finally sunk in. Ronald stroked his fake mustache while Josh drummed his fingers on his thigh. After at least three minutes of dead quiet, they turned to face each other.

"So the secret to being impressive," Ronald said, "is to act like you don't even want to be impressive."

"You took the words right out of my mouth!" Josh agreed.

"AGGGGGH!" I yelled. "You're not getting it!"

Next to me I heard the cold sound of metal sliding against metal.

"Of course, he's not getting it," said

a voice drenched in sarcasm. It was the guard, talking through the slat in the door. "According to the *Bay City Gazette*, he's no more clever than the orangutans who saved his life in that boring movie. He's got much less personality too."

I squeezed the vial of sleeping potion tight. It was time to act.

39

Coffee... Ground!

The guard leaned down to peer through the slot in the door. He had a face like a ham that had been boiled in dishwater.

"I heard the boss talking," he said. "His master plan ends very, *very* badly for you kids."

"What about me?" Josh demanded.

The buffoon snorted. "The boss didn't say anything about you. I think he agrees with the *Bay City Gazette* that 'Brigand's work is light on ideas and even lighter on originality.'"

The guard took a long slurp of coffee. Julianne stood with her back pressed against the door, where the guard couldn't see her. She kept the sleeping serum squeezed in her fist. The cold fluorescent lights flickered overhead.

"Do you know who you're dealing with?" I asked.

The guard took another noisy drink of coffee, smacking his lips. "You have about as much chance of escape as Brigand does of having anyone like his movie."

He set his coffee mug down on the tray outside our door and snapped open a newspaper.

"'The film is as bloated as a dead fish,'" he read, cackling. "'And far less fun to spend three hours with.'"

His laughs echoed through the brig, then we heard the heels of his shoes click away, down the hall. Once he'd gone a few steps, Julianne dove for the door, with the vial open. She checked to see if the coast was clear, before pulling away.

"He's walking toward us again," she said, sliding out of sight.

I could hear our jailer's shoes clicking back in our direction.

"'The love story would have been better off between Brigand and his character's pet parrot,'" he continued between rough little chuckles. "'Who else could tolerate the actor's phony swagger?'"

Josh groaned as the guard picked up his coffee cup, took another noisy slurp, and set it back down. He clicked off in the other direction a second time.

"'The underused lead actress and a scene with trained orangutans were the lone bright spots in an otherwise boring . . .'"

Julianne snaked her hand out of the slot and tipped a few drops of the sleeping serum into the mug, then pulled her hand back in again and ran to the bed to sit next to Josh, wiping the sweat off her forehead.

"I hope I added enough," she whispered.

It wasn't long before the guard reappeared, still giggling over the review, for another drink of coffee. The second he set the mug back down, my partner in dazzling schemes spoke.

"Your coffee was poisoned," she said. Her voice was calm and steady—only a fool would dare ignore it. "And we have the antidote. You have probably . . . One minute to get in here and get it from us before the poison takes hold."

The guard pressed his boiled-ham face right up against the slot in the door. Julianne sat on the bed and waggled the vial at him.

"We put it in the mug when your back was turned."

"Nonsense," the guard stammered.

"I told you the Danger Gang would rescue me," Brigand said with a smile. "Feeling sleepy yet?"

There was silence out in the hall, and I knew that the guard had begun to weaken. I could imagine the color slowly draining from his pink face.

"Okeeee," he slurred. "Gimmmmmeee that antidooooo."

"You have to come in and get it, you devilish varlet," I said. "And you'll probably want to hurry. Sato, how long do you think he has?"

"Thirty seconds now," Julianne said, "maybe less."

We could hear the villain's keys jangling as he raced to open the door. I beamed at my friends.

"The plan is going off without a hitch," I whispered excitedly.

Then the hall echoed with a heavy thud and the tinkling of metal keys on the floor.

"Well, *there's* a hitch for you," Julianne said.

FACT: The guard had collapsed before he could get the door open.

I raced across the room and pressed my face to the open slat. Sure enough, the coffee had grounded the scalawag. He was zonked out on the cold iron floor, with his chest rising and falling evenly, letting out little wet-sounding snores with each breath.

His keys were on the floor beside him. I backed away from the door and Julianne took my place. Brigand stood in the middle of the room, confused.

I pressed my face against the door slat
and saw the guard sprawled on the ground.
I must've gone a little heavy on the
sleeping serum. There was clanking and noise
behind us, and I glanced over my shoulder.

Ronald had thrown the mattress off the cot and was busy unwinding one of the bedsprings. He stretched it until it looked like a long, metal noodle, and then he bent a hook at the end.

"Stand back," he said. "Ronald Zupan has an idea!"

I was just about to pull away from the slat so that Ronald could fish for the keys with the bedspring when I heard a loud banging overhead. Down the hall, at the very edge of my sightline, I saw the outline of an air vent. Someone was stomping on it from the inside.

THUNK! THUNK! THUNK! THUNK!

The metal covering fell and clanked against the ground. Seconds later, someone dressed in all black swung out the vent, landing lightly on the floor. Suddenly, the hall went black.

Josh gasped. "What in the—"

"Quiet Brigand, someone's in the brig," Ronald said.

A flashlight beam started to dance around

the hallway, and I ran back to stand in the dark with my friends. Next, we heard the guard's keys clink together. There was another pause . . . and our cell door slid open.

The flashlight shone on us standing in the corner. A figure stood silhouetted at the door.

"Who are you?" Ronald demanded.

He pulled back his arm with the bedspring, as if it were a bullwhip. The person at the door flipped the flashlight around. Now, it illuminated a narrow face with high cheekbones and dark hair tied up in a bun. She started to speak, but I had the words out first.

"The woman in the cape," I said aloud.

40

Capes and Escapes!

The woman in the cape stared at us. With the flashlight held under her chin, she looked ghostly. "I wondered if you'd spotted me on the hill. We've been searching for the same person. You found him first"—she smiled—"but I managed to do it without getting caught."

I looked over at Brigand. Even in the dark I could see his jaw hanging open to reveal his bright white molars.

"I-Isa," he stammered. "What are you doing here?"

The woman reached her arms back to pull a pin out of her bun and shook out her long dark hair. "I'm rescuing you. Though you hardly deserve it."

Julianne turned toward me. "Ronald, do you have any idea what—"

"None at all," I said, dropping the bedspring. "Zero."

Brigand stood up and stepped forward a little. "Uh . . . Julianne, Ronald, meet Isabella Montoya. You might recognize her as Queen Esmeralda from *Buccaneers of the South Seas*."

"They'd have to watch quite closely," the woman scoffed. "All my good scenes were taken out."

Without much light, it was hard to tell, but she certainly *seemed* like a movie star. Her shoulders were proud and her black hair shone, even in the darkness.

"Wait," Julianne said, "so you chased us from outside the theater, across the ocean, onto Capstone Island, over to the cliffs . . ."

"I was behind you most of the time," Isabella said, "so I can see how it looked like I was chasing you. But I was simply following the kidnappers."

I stroked my dashing mustache until it fluttered to the floor. "Wait, Isabella—"

"Call me Isa. All my friends do."

"Okay, Isa," I said, "but why were you waiting outside the movie theater instead of coming in to see the premiere?"

"Yes, *Isa*," Brigand said, his voice growing hard, "why didn't you come in?"

"*You* should call me Isabella," Isa said sharply, rolling her shoulders back. "And I didn't come inside because a friend at the studio told me I was hardly in the final movie. As for why I was at Bay City Cinema . . ." She hesitated. "I had a

plan. It seems silly now, but . . . I was going to swing onto the red carpet after the movie let out, using a grappling hook."

"No plan that uses grappling hooks is silly," I said.

Isa looked at me and Julianne instead of Josh. "The idea was that the Capstone Pictures people would see that I could do my own stunts. But no one stuck around after the movie, so there was no point." She finally turned to Josh again. "I was sitting in my car, getting ready to give you a piece of my mind, when you got abducted."

"So you followed the kidnappers?" Brigand asked.

"You're not great," Isa said. "But even *you* don't deserve to be kidnapped by men with stun guns."

Brigand shifted uncomfortably.

Julianne looked between the two of them, then turned to me. "Talk about a twist."

Isa ran her flashlight beam across me, Julianne, and Josh. "We have to get off the ship."

The four of us ducked out of the cell. The guard was still snoring and didn't show any signs of waking up. I snatched his key ring out of our door and unlocked the other two cells.

My father stepped out of his cell with Jeeves by his side. "That was quicker than I expected." He peered at Isa in the half-light. "And who is this caped woman?"

"It's kind of a long story," Julianne said as I unlocked the next cell. "She was in Josh's movie."

"Barely," Isa grumbled.

My mother left her cell with Mr. Sato. I explained what had happened to the four of them.

"Julianne, that was a good idea with the coffee," my mother said, tossing her gray-haired wig on the ground. "And Ronald, smart thinking with the bedspring."

Mr. Sato stooped down and found a small flashlight hanging from the guard's belt. He unclipped it and flipped it on. "Does anyone have an idea for where to go next?"

"I'd say getting off this ship is in order," Jeeves said.

Brigand made a face like he'd just eaten a puffer fish. "The FIB has twenty men with guns, and we have . . . what *do* we have?"

"Swords!" I said. "The most noble weapon an adventurer can own!"

I ran down the hall and rooted around on the guard's desk for our rapiers. The satchel was there too, and I grabbed it, even though all it had left inside were two tins of anchovies and one polo mallet.

Isa shone her flashlight around the hall. "We can't go back up into the air vents."

"We'll have to try to sneak past—" Julianne stopped when she noticed Mr. Sato motioning to her with his flashlight.

The second I stepped toward my grandfather, I realized he might not be thrilled with me.

"Ojii-chan, I'm sorry," I said. "I had to try to rescue Josh. He's my friend."

"I know," he said. There was a long pause. "Still ... I was scared."

His words put a lump in my throat. I hadn't meant to scare him. I stepped forward and leaned my head on his shoulder. He wrapped me up tighter than I expected. After a second, I tried to make a joke.

"I thought you were going to ground me," I said. "Heh, heh!"

He kept hugging me. "Oh, you're definitely grounded. No doubt about it."

He was sort of chuckling, which was confusing.

"Wait ..." I said. "I can't tell if you're joking, or—"

"Very serious," he said. "Grounded for at least a month. We can talk about it back home."

Francisco snatched the nightstick off the FIB guard's belt, spun it in his hand a few times, and led the way out of the brig.

"Hold on," Isa said.

Everyone turned. She swept back her cape to reveal a sword sheathed at her waist.

"I should go ahead."

My father hesitated, then made room for her. "Julianne and Ronald, you guard the rear. These scalawags may sneak up from behind, just like the terrifying tiger beetle."

41

Lost in the Shuffle!

We crept up the circular iron staircase, toward the ball-room level, where we'd been captured.

"Sato," I whispered, "I'd like to note that I recognized the Brasher Doubloon because I'd seen it in Death Valley. So the trip *was* worthwhile."

I took a few more stairs, glancing behind us every few seconds.

"How do you figure?" she asked.

"It helped me recognize Snidewater," I said.

Jeeves was in front of Julianne, and he turned around. "You recognized him literally one second before his men jumped us. You saved maybe one second, right?"

There was no time to explain to him that one second can make a world of difference in the life of a master adventurer.

We'd arrived at a little alcove, with just enough space for all of us to stand, and a door on either side. One door opened into the gambling pit, and the other opened out on the deck of the ship.

With the six of us crowded behind her, Isa slowly creaked open the iron door to the deck, then pulled it shut again almost instantly.

"We are on the wrong side of the ship," she said. "This isn't where the boats are tied up."

"We could sneak around the deck," Mr. Sato suggested.

Isa shook her head. "There are two guards with a spotlight. They'd see us."

"The second we're seen, it's sure to cause a scene," my mother muttered.

We stayed huddled at the top of the stairs.

"I believe," my father said, stroking his beard, "we're going to have to scurry across the ballroom floor, just like a family of hissing cockroaches."

With the rest of us at his back, he cracked the second door, which opened onto the gambling pit. We heard Snidewater's voice immediately.

"Men and women of the FIB," the feared villain snarled into a microphone, "downstairs, I have the movie star Josh Brigand locked in a cell. Using him, I've lured all three members of the Danger Gang—the same trio that bested Zeetan Z in Borneo—onto this ship. Not only that, but we also captured the world-famous Helen and Francisco Zupan, plus an elderly accomplice."

Francisco cracked the door a little farther, and we peered down toward the other end of the ballroom. The view was mostly blocked, but between pillars and tall flower arrangements we could see flashes of Snidewater on the stage, addressing his men.

"We did this all one night before we expected," he said. "*While* running a floating casino!"

The crowd cheered.

"By defeating our enemies in dramatic fashion, *we* are next in line to lead the entire Liars' Club!"

The odor-infested crew stomped and whistled.

"I can't hear you!" Snidewater said.

The FIB roared twice as loud as before.

"*I. Can't. Hear. You!*" Snidewater screamed, making the microphone squeal with feedback.

This time the crowd flew into a wild frenzy. They chanted "F-I-B! F-I-B!" and stomped so hard that it rattled the chandeliers.

"Now," my mother whispered.

Francisco slipped out the door, crawled across the carpet, and rolled behind one of the card tables. Isa went after him, and Mr. Sato after her. Helen was next, then Jeeves, Julianne, and me.

"Boss," a thin, nasally voice called, "does that mean we

get to have the big fireworks show tonight instead of waiting for tomorrow?"

"Who cares about fireworks?" Snidewater said over the microphone. "The point is that I'm the new leader of the largest criminal organization in the world! My power is unmatched! Zeetan Z can never tease me again! I am a legend!"

This time no one cheered. After a minute, we heard grumbles from a few of the FIB crew.

"What?" Snidewater snapped. "What is it?"

Another pause.

"Well," a voice piped up, "*we* were really hoping for the fireworks."

"Yeah," another voice called, "I mean . . . to celebrate your victory over your archenemy and all."

We sneaked across the room, one person at a time, lying flat on the red carpet and diving behind the tables to take cover.

By the time Jeeves, Julianne, and I ducked behind the first table, Isa and Mr. Sato had wriggled across the carpet and slid out the door at the far side of the room. Unless someone was standing watch on that side of the ship, they'd be in a boat in no time.

"You want the fireworks?" Snidewater asked.

The FIB exploded into cheers and my father used the opening to wave my mother and Josh Brigand forward.

"Fine," the scoundrel said. "Fink, Snibble, go get the fireworks from the forward hold and bring them up on the deck. We'll have our fireworks show. To celebrate our reign as leaders of the Liars' Club. To celebrate the fact that the pirate Zeetan Z can never mock the FIB again."

A door slammed near the front of the room as two crewmembers sprinted off to get the fireworks. The crowd of villains chanted their leader's name.

"Tonight," Snidewater said, "we light Roman candles to celebrate! We have been disrespected for too long. Now *everyone* will fear us."

More cheers.

"This dastardly dog has no idea who he's dealing with," I whispered to my friends as we got ready to crawl to the next table. "He's . . ."

I was looking over my shoulder at Julianne and Jeeves, so I didn't see what happened next—I just saw their faces fill with dread.

FACT: I braced myself for catastrophe.

It wasn't Josh's fault. Not really. A cord from an electric card-shuffling machine caught on his foot as he crawled across the floor. Jeeves and I saw it, but there was no time to stop what was happening.

CRASH!

The shuffling machine slammed to the floor and spit a deck of cards high into the air. For a second, it was silent. We had time to cross our fingers that no one noticed.

Then Snidewater screamed, "Someone's hiding back there!"

We heard the stomping of FIB footsteps as the men charged us. A moment later, the door down to the brig burst open. It was the guard I'd given the sleeping serum to. From my hiding spot, I caught a glance of him. He looked wide-awake and spitting mad.

"The captives have escaped!" he yelled.

42

Going Overboard!

Snidewater was still onstage, screaming into the microphone. *"They're in the gambling pit! Seize them!"*

From our spot behind the table, we saw Francisco, Helen, and Josh all spring to their feet. My father grabbed a tray of poker chips from one of the gambling tables and flung them at an approaching crowd of henchmen. Then he stepped into fencing stance, twirling the billy club he'd stolen off the guard's belt.

I jumped up too, but iron fingers snared my ankle and dragged me back to the floor. I rolled over, kicking to get free. It was Jeeves—he had one hand holding me and the other on Julianne.

"Let us go!" I said. "What . . . are . . . you . . . . *doing?*"

"We're outnumbered," Jeeves whispered. "We can only help by staying hidden."

From my spot on the floor, I saw twenty members of the FIB whip pistols out of their jackets. They had my parents and Josh totally surrounded.

"Ha," my father scoffed. "Only the most classless villains use guns. Fight fair, you rogues."

Jeeves scooted backward, out of sight, dragging Julianne and me under the cover of a tablecloth.

"*Surrender!*" Snidewater bellowed from the stage.

"We *will* surrender!" my father boomed back. He paused for dramatic effect. "But only when the FIB learns to floss their teeth. Which is *never!*"

We peeked out to see what was happening just as my mother stepped forward.

"Actually, darling," she said softly, "they have us surrounded. Besides, the Danger Gang is long gone . . . listen, you can hear their boat buzzing away."

Jeeves, Julianne, and I tucked together tightly under the table, covered by the tablecloth, hoping desperately that no one had seen us.

Josh Brigand caught Helen's lie right away.

"Right you are," he said. "I *can* hear their boat. They're probably already in radio range of the Bay City police."

"Now *that's* good acting," I whispered to my friends.

I lay flat on the carpet and lifted up the tablecloth on the other side of the table, just the tiniest bit. I could see a set of boots ten feet away, right by the door to the brig. If we could get back there, we'd be able to sneak downstairs again, or out onto the deck.

"Droggle!" Snidewater called. "Stop looking like a sap and come here! Explain yourself!"

After a moment of hesitation, the boots shuffled out of sight. We had a clear path now, and the door was wide open. We just had to make it there without being seen.

"They said they put something in my coffee, boss," the man named Droggle explained. "The next thing I knew, I woke up on the floor."

Snidewater's voice was cold and sinister. "And *how* did they get your coffee to put something in it?"

Droggle stuttered through a reply.

"Speak up," Snidewater said with his mouth so close to the microphone that it made a strange popping sound.

"I left it on the food tray outside the cell door," Droggle said. "So that I could read Brigand's terrible reviews to him."

"*You idiot!*" Snidewater roared. The room filled with the crash of shattering plates.

"In his defense," came Francisco's voice from the other side of the gambling pit, "the Danger Gang is known for their clever plots and dazzling schemes."

"Enjoy feeling clever now," Snidewater said. "Soon you'll be in far too much pain to think of cleverness."

"Boss, what do you want us to do with Brigand and the Zupans?" a voice called.

"Bring them here," Snidewater said into the microphone,

his voice brimming with hatred. "And I want a boat in each direction to chase down the Danger Gang!"

FACT: My mother's scheme had worked!

The room was filled with the sounds of movement as a group of villains rushed out the door to the boats. I knew that Isa and Mr. Sato were out there somewhere, but I doubted the FIB would be able to find them. Inside, another group of goons dragged my parents and Josh Brigand toward the front of the gambling ship. It was clear that the three of them were fighting the scalawags every inch—kicking over platters and wrestling to shake free.

This was enough commotion for Jeeves, Julianne, and me to slip out from under the table and back into the alcove at the top of the staircase.

"We can't go downstairs again," Julianne said once we'd eased the door closed. "We'd be trapped."

The second door, leading onto the ship's deck, was still the tiniest bit open from when Isa had peeked outside. I cracked it another few centimeters and saw the two watchmen. They were scanning the horizon with a spotlight.

"All right," I whispered to Jeeves, "time to slow down and think through our options, just like you're always saying."

Jeeves looked at me. "Thank you for that, Ronald, but this actually feels like a time to act without thinking."

With a strange smirk, Jeeves slammed the door with his shoulder and raced onto the deck with his polo mallet whirling. Ronald and I started to follow him, but before we could even get out the door, he'd pounced on the two watchmen and they both went soaring over the rail.

Jeeves turned to us, brushing a stray strand of hair away from his forehead and flattening down a few of the medals on the lapel of his jacket.

"Well," he said as the men wailed and slapped the water down below, "now what?"

Julianne held up a hand for quiet. Someone was coming in our direction. We waited, weapons at the ready, and after another second we could hear snatches of a conversation.

"What do you think the boss will do to the Danger Gang?" a voice asked between heaving breaths.

"Sharks?" a second voice wondered. "Maybe worse. *I* sure wouldn't want to be his archenemy."

Clearly these voices belonged to Fink and Snibble, the two men Snidewater had sent to find the crate of fireworks. We could hear them dragging it across the iron deck of the ship.

Julianne, Jeeves, and I all pressed our backs against the wall, waiting. A second later, the two FIB cronies came into view. The crate they were dragging was huge, and they could only wrestle it across the deck a few feet at a time.

When Fink and Snibble were about ten feet away, the taller man stopped. Something had caught his eye. He peered out over the railing of the ship and his partner rushed to join him. They cupped their hands and started to yell.

"*What are you two doing down there?*" one of the men called.

It was obvious that the two lookouts Jeeves had knocked overboard were trying to swim around to the front of the ship, so they could climb back aboard the gangplank. Now the four FIB rogues screamed back and forth in the darkness while we kept as quiet as Bolivian field mice.

The men in the water yelled something that we couldn't decipher.

"*The cat hid our shoes?*" the tall man said.

He was wearing a crimson tuxedo, like all the card dealers on the ship, but the pants were three inches too short. I had a feeling this one was Fink.

Both FIB henchmen had their backs to us. Without a word, Jeeves, Julianne, and I started to creep forward.

"*What cat?*" the second man yelled down at his compatriots. He had a squat, round body; a bald, round head; and almost no neck between the two. He seemed like a "Snibble" if ever there was one.

The men in the water yelled again.

"I think it's the cat hid our *loose*," Snibble muttered.

By this time Julianne and I had snuck up right behind the two men, with our sword tips almost touching their backs.

Jeeves cleared his throat. "I believe they're yelling 'the captives are loose,'" he said, straightening up so that the medals on his coat tinkled together.

Fink and Snibble wheeled around to find themselves staring down two razor-sharp rapiers.

FACT: They knew they were beat; it showed on their faces.

Julianne motioned overboard with her head and the two men both shivered. They gave the crate of fireworks one last longing look, sighed, and lifted themselves onto the rail of the ship. With a deep breath they leaped into the swirling, dark water below.

SPLASH! SPLASH!

"That's four down," I said as the two FIB henchmen dog-paddled toward their friends. "It'll take them at least ten minutes to swim around to the other side of the ship. Now's the time to make our move."

"Ronald," Julianne said, patting the top of the crate, "I think we should have a new addition to our code . . . Something like: 'The Danger Gang isn't afraid to use fireworks to strike down villains.'"

"Sato," I said, "I love it. Jeeves, where do you stand on fireworks as weapons?"

A few nails groaned as Jeeves wrenched the lid off the crate. He grabbed a Roman candle and smiled. "Sounds like a plan."

43

Fighting Fire with Fireworks!

The crate was packed with Roman candles and bottle rockets, plus entire bags of sparklers, smoke bombs, pop-its, and those strange little black disks that stretch into writhing worms.

I grabbed a fistful of firecrackers. "Now we just need a way to light them."

I rooted through the satchel. The matches were gone but my eyes soon settled on an electrical box bolted to the wall. It was a circuit board, and it looked big enough to run the electricity for the whole ship.

"Friends," I said, "I have an idea for how we can get a fire started *and* give ourselves the element of surprise."

I stepped to the electrical box and flipped the clamps holding it shut.

"Jeeves," I said, "some help."

The good butler gave a firm nod, spun his polo mallet twice, and smashed the panel with all his might. The circuits started to smoke and the smell of melting wires filled the air.

We all took a step backward and the circuit board gave a giant *POP!* The pieces split apart, and a fire started to crackle. After one more pop the entire ship was cast in darkness. The electricity was out everywhere.

"Now," I told my friends, "take all the fireworks you can carry."

We tucked as many bottle rockets, smoke bombs, and Roman candles as we could in every pocket we had. I crumpled up a wad of straw from the crate and walked over to the fizzling electrical box. It lit in seconds.

I dropped the smoking bundle of straw on the iron deck of the ship before it caught flame. When the first fistful of straw turned to ash, I tossed some more on the pile. Jeeves wrenched three boards off the crate. We held them over the fire until each board had a bright red ember burning on the end.

I started to open my mouth with a plan, but Julianne beat me to it.

"I'll go for the captives," she said, blowing on her ember until it gave off a little twist of smoke. "Jeeves, you make a distraction. Ronald"—she motioned to an iron ladder with the tip of her smoldering board—"you go into the rafters and attack the FIB from above. That seems very Ronald-ish, right?"

"I like the word 'Zupanian' better," I said. "But yes."

The ladder led up to the roof of the ship's second level. There was a row of glass-paned windows overhead, and I figured that was where to access the catwalks. I grabbed the first rung of the ladder and started to climb, then turned back to my brave compatriots.

"Friends," I said, "remember when I mutinied?"

Julianne shrugged. "I mean . . . it only lasted about an hour, but yeah."

Jeeves nodded. "Even less. Forty minutes, tops. It was a *very* short mutiny."

"The point is," I said, climbing a little farther up the ladder, "it was my least favorite part of this whole adventure. I like it best when we're all a team."

I didn't wait for them to answer, just scurried up the ladder to the second level of the stern-wheeler with my smoldering piece of wood in one hand. At the top, there was a narrow ridge and a row of smoky windows. Beyond them, I could just barely make out the catwalks, where FIB lackeys had rained down balloons and confetti a few hours earlier.

I used my sword to slowly pry open a locked window. Then I eased silently onto the first platform. I sheathed my sword so that I could hold the piece of smoldering wood in one hand and shield it from sight with the other. My clothes sagged under the weight of fireworks.

"*What is going on with the lights?*" I heard Snidewater snarl. "*Someone fix them!*"

The FIB goons started stumbling around in the dark. Finally, one of them found a few flashlights—their weak beams bounced around the ballroom. My father's voice cut through the darkness.

"This can't be going how you hoped," he said to Snidewater. "Half your captives are missing, and your ship is under siege."

"*Oh shut up!*" Snidewater screamed. "Nothing has changed. I'll still defeat the Danger Gang and be the leader of the entire Liars' Club. I'll be feared the world over—the way Zeetan Z was feared! More even! I'll never be ignored again!"

"You're a villain with no conscience," my mother said. "I can't wait till my son and his friends knock unconscious."

It wasn't her best wordplay, but it made me proud to hear that she believed in me, and her steady voice calmed my racing nerves.

"The Danger Gang?" Snidewater spat. "Two of them are children! My men will capture them before they ever reach shore."

"What if they never left the ship at all?" my father said. "Maybe they are just waiting to attack you, like a funnel-web spider."

Snidewater stepped close to my father; they were nose to nose. His flashlight beam made both of their faces glow.

"Listen close, Zupan," he said, "I'm going to chum the

water for sharks, then throw you and your wife over-board. So maybe you should worry more about being scared yourself."

"We'll escape first!" Josh Brigand grunted from some-where nearby. I could tell he was struggling to wrestle free of whoever was holding him.

I shuffled along the catwalks until I was right above Snidewater and my father, looking down at their shadowy figures.

"Shut up, Brigand," Snidewater called. "Your movie failed; your dreams of escaping will fail too."

FACT: For the first time in my life, I felt protective of Josh Brigand.

I drew a Roman candle out of my jacket. It was easy enough to know where our enemies were—most of them had scrounged up flashlights by now, and the ones who hadn't were chattering nervously.

I held the red tip of the board toward the wick of the Roman candle and paused. Snidewater was too close to my parents to get a clear shot.

Meanwhile, I was kneeling down at the base of the stage, just a few feet away from

Snidewater, the Zupans, and Josh. FIB members were shuffling around the dark ballroom while their leader mocked his captives.

Two men walked right past me, waving their flashlights in dark corners, wondering aloud what had happened to the lights, when a massive crash came from the gambling pit. Jeeves had knocked over one of the blackjack tables and the chips tinkled across the floor. He knocked over another, then another. He was stumbling through the darkness to each table and flipping it over with a crash.

"What's going on now?" Snidewater bellowed. I peeked over the ridge of the stage, and there was just enough light from all the flashlights to see the dark outline of his pistol in one hand.

"Take this, you yellow-bellied rogue!" I heard Ronald scream from above.

A purple ball of fire shot down and hit Snidewater's hand. The gun clacked down on the stage. Before the FIB leader could reach for it, another fireball rocketed toward him. The villain dove for cover and I saw my chance. I hopped up onto the stage and crawled toward where I'd heard the Zupans' voices.

A yellow star from a second Roman candle soared through the ballroom from the gambling pit and caught in the giant velvet curtain behind the stage. Flames licked the fabric and started to climb higher.

"The boy is in the catwalks!" Snidewater yelled from some dark corner. "Get him!"

I could hear some of his men clanking their way up a ladder and knew that Ronald was trapped. The room was glowing now with bursts of sparks from fireworks over my head. I crawled to Josh first and cut him free with my sword, then freed Helen and Francisco.

"Quick," I yelled to them, "Ronald's in trouble!"

44

The Gang in Danger!

I used my smoldering piece of wood to light two more Roman candles, sending jets of sparks rocketing toward the rogues.

FSSST! FSSSSSSST!

Each new blast of yellow or purple scared my enemies for a moment, but the FIB thugs had scaled ladders around the ballroom and were closing in on me from all sides.

"I need some help up here!" I screamed, hoping my friends would hear me.

"It's no picnic down here, either!" Julianne answered back.

Clearly, I was on my own for the moment. To my left, I saw a pinched-faced man slinking toward me.

"Surrender now," he said, his nose twitching in the glow of his flashlight. "And maybe the boss won't hurt you . . . *much.*"

I backed up a few steps to get away from the fiend, but there was no place to go. I fired Roman candles—brilliant bursts of yellow, green, and blue—but the rogues simply brushed the sparks off their jackets and trudged forward, reaching toward me with their arms wide. Even in the chaos, I could see that a few of the men had guns drawn.

"Ronald," my father bellowed from below, "the balloons!"

"The wha—"

My eyes caught on a net dangling over the ballroom, about four feet from where I stood. It was full of balloons waiting to rain down on revelers aboard the Serpent of the Mist.

> **FACT: I knew exactly what Francisco wanted me to do.**

"Charge!" the pinched-faced man yelled, and FIB members raced at me, their steps clanging across the catwalks. I spun in a circle, firing a jet of Roman candle sparks at each of them, then stood up on the guardrail, wavered for a second, and leaped over to the net of balloons.

I grabbed the top of the net, wobbled dangerously, and hung on like a terrified lemur. As the FIB leaned over the rail, trying to grab me, I slashed at the ropes that held the whole net high in the rafters.

I heard Ronald yelling before I saw him. By the time I spun toward the sound, he was dropping from the catwalk. When the balloon-filled net hit the ground, it flattened out and absorbed the impact, which I think Ronald was counting on. But the force sent him shooting off toward the stage, which I don't think he expected.

He landed with a thud and a sharp cry of pain.

There was a terrible pop and more explosions of color, this time inside my head. My left arm had come right out of the socket. I rose to my feet and it sort of dangled there, useless. Heat radiated from my shoulder down to my tingling fingertips.

Blasts from Roman candles flew every direction. The FIB must have found the crate and Snidewater's low-level thugs fired at us from all sides. The shadow of a tall skinny man ducked toward me. He grabbed my shoulder and I let out the

scream of a very brave adventurer simply greeting a friend, not drowning in complete and total agony.

"What happened?" Jeeves asked.

"It's out of the socket," I said.

"No time to deal with it now; we have to get off the ship. There are too many of them."

He glanced at the burning curtain behind the stage. The ballroom was starting to flood with smoke. I spotted my parents a few feet away, trying to force Snidewater into a corner. Julianne and Josh were back-to-back behind a pillar, fending off three FIB devils.

"Everyone!" Jeeves called. "This way!"

We all ran toward Jeeves, and he passed Roman candles to my parents and Josh, while Julianne and I held off the FIB.

"To the boats!" my father yelled.

We raced out the side doors of the ship and sprinted for the floating dock. Julianne and I were in the lead, with Josh, Helen, Francisco, and Jeeves five steps behind us. As we skidded across the deck, another set of doors flew open and ten FIB members stepped out of the ballroom. They separated Julianne and me from the others.

"Over here!" a woman's voice yelled from below.

It was Isa Montoya and Mr. Sato in the Zupan speedboat. They turned hard, sent a wall of spray into the air, and pulled up right below where Jeeves, Josh, and my parents all stood. Half of the FIB goons were running at them. The other half charged straight for me and Julianne.

45

No Place Like Hode!

I slammed the throttle of our boat down as hard as I could and Julianne lit her last two Roman candles. The first one she aimed at Snidewater and Deadly Dirk, but the second she held up so that each burst of sparks exploded in the night sky. We could only hope that someone would see them and know we needed help.

"Yes!" Julianne yelled. "I just hit Dirk Grimple right in the chest."

"Did he go overboard?" I asked.

Julianne didn't answer for a second. "Ugh. He's on his feet again. How did he even *get* to the Serpent?"

"Maybe they had a patch kit for their life raft," I said.

"Well, whatever new boat he found is fast," Julianne replied. "It's closing in."

A red streak of light flew past my shoulder and hit the windshield of our skiff. A white one hit a seat and started to smolder. Julianne slapped it with a corner of her dress.

"I'm out of fireworks," she said.

I gritted my teeth. "I only have those little ash worms."

Julianne stood beside me but faced backward. "We're a hundred feet ahead of them, but . . ."

I knew what was coming before she even finished.

"They're gaining on us," I said.

Our boat skipped across the waves, throttle jammed as far as it could go. The motor droned so loud that we had to yell to hear each other. Up ahead, I could just make out the shadowy monstrous shapes of the cliffs at Hode Point. That meant the theater was to our left.

"I have to turn now if we're going toward the harbor," I said. "If they see us turn, they'll cut diagonally and—"

There was a look of despair on my adventure partner's face. It told me everything.

"We won't make it, will we?" I asked over the sound of the bow bouncing off the waves.

For the first time, I risked turning completely toward her just as a yellow star, shot from a mortar, exploded above our heads and showered us with sparks.

"No," Julianne said, "we won't make it."

"Time for plan B," Ronald said.

He veered toward the back of Capstone Island and aimed the bow of our boat at the towering cliffs. I knew the iron ladders would be slick with dew. I knew the door to the tunnels would be locked. I even knew that the Brothers Grin might be waiting.

But there was one more thing I knew: we didn't have any choice. Heading to Hode Point was our only hope.

Another massive mortar exploded right above our heads. The sparks spiraled and spiderwebbed across the sky. A few of them fell in my hair; I had to lean over the side of the boat to splash water on top of my head.

"Sato," Ronald said, "I need you to do me a favor. And it's not going to be fun."

"What is it?" I asked. I wondered if he could hear the panic in my voice. I wondered if he knew how terrified I was.

"I need you to jam my shoulder back into the socket," he said. "I'll never be able to climb those ladders with one arm."

"Is it going to hurt?" I asked, stepping toward him.

He forced a half grin through gritted teeth. "Ronald Zupan is incredibly resistant to pain," he said. "But this . . . this will probably hurt."

Julianne wrapped both hands around my upper arm. I'd never had my shoulder pop out of socket, but I'd heard stories. It had happened to Helen while she was sailing down the Ganges River.

"So . . . just jam it back into place?" Julianne asked.

"Indeed," I said.

She rolled her bottom lip between her teeth. "If you say so."

We were interrupted by another explosion of sparks. They hit our motor and skittered across the boat. Julianne had to rush around stomping them out. Snidewater and Deadly Dirk were closing in: less than fifty feet away.

"Here goes," Julianne said, stepping into place.

She tried to push my shoulder into the socket, but she was too gentle. It was enough to send a wave of searing pain through me, but not enough to help the problem.

"Agggggggh! *Harder!*" I yelled.

Julianne tried again. It hurt worse this time, but my shoulder still didn't pop back in. I needed to do something to make her really push.

I turned to her, my eyes watering. "Sato," I said, "I secretly still think of myself as leader of the Danger—"

FACT: That was all it took! She popped my shoulder in with so much force that I felt it in my molars.

"Thank you!" I groaned as the pain in my arm faded a bit. "Now . . . get ready for the climb of your life."

I could hear Snidewater and Grimple's boat roaring across the waves behind us. The wall was ahead—a sheer slab of rock, disappearing into the clouds. The moon filtered through the mist and I spotted the ladders. They seemed to stretch skyward for miles.

"I'm going to come into the dock at full speed," I yelled. "We'll have to jump and climb!"

Julianne started flinging open storage compartments and filling both of our pockets with anything heavy she could find—a screwdriver, a small fire extinguisher, a spool of wire.

I slid into the dock sideways and we leaped ashore. There were at least ten ladders, connected by iron platforms, before we'd be at the top. Julianne grabbed the first rung and started racing skyward. I was right on her heels, wincing every time I had to use my left arm.

"We'll need a big head start to beat them up the ladders,"

Julianne huffed, when she made it to the second platform. "At least three minutes."

I risked a glance over my shoulder. "We're going to have to settle for a lot less than that," I said, panting for breath. "Snidewater and Grimple just started climbing."

46

The Edge of Disaster!

Dirk Grimple and Snidewater started closing the gap almost instantly. By the time we hit the halfway point, the two scalawags were only fifty feet below us.

Julianne let me go ahead and threw the fire extinguisher down at them. It bounced off a ladder, spraying foam everywhere as it tumbled past Deadly Dirk. The spool of wire hit Snidewater on the shoulder but didn't faze him.

I tried to use only my right hand to climb, but sometimes I had to brace myself with my left and it sent waves of pain through my arm every time. I was slowing us down and I knew it.

"Julianne, let's turn and fight them on one of these platforms," I said, struggling for breath. "We're fencing experts."

"They're . . . bigger than . . . us," Julianne panted.

"And . . . in close quarters . . . I'm not sure . . . we'd beat them."

Especially with you hurt, I finished for her, inside my head.

I gritted my teeth through the pain and kept going. We had to get to the top. We could defeat them out in the open. Or at least we had a better chance.

By the time we got to the last ladder, our enemies were on our heels. We could hear them grunting just a few rungs below us.

Julianne was still behind me, and when I stood up on the lip of the cliff, she shrieked. Dirk Grimple had her ankle in his vise grip. He was trying to yank her off the ladder. I whipped out my sword and drove the point into the fleshy part of his hand. He roared in agony and jerked away, almost falling on Snidewater.

Julianne pulled away from the villain and scrambled up onto the cliff. The second she was standing, her breathing hitched.

"Ronald," she said, "look."

I turned around. The Brothers Grin stood twenty feet away, arms crossed, satisfied smiles on their faces. Their Jeep was running, parked on a slope, and inside we could see someone tied up and fighting to get loose. Elias.

"We saw your signal," Jake Grin said, "and we're very excited to meet you again."

"And so soon after catching this sniveling runt in the tunnels!" Bill Grin echoed, his mustache twitching.

The Jeep's headlights caught in the fog and cast the cliff in an eerie glow. Up on the nearby ridges, I could just make out the eyes of hundreds of fennec foxes, watching us.

In the time it took for us to see the Brothers Grin, Snidewater and Dirk Grimple climbed up on the cliff. Now, we found ourselves outnumbered, exhausted, and—in Ronald's case—fighting with a hurt shoulder.
The odds didn't look good.

Dirk Grimple swept back his coat to reveal a sword slung on each hip. He drew one for himself and handed the other to Snidewater.

"Here you go, boss," he said. "Time to defeat your archenemy."

Snidewater took it and began edging toward us. He was a fencer, you could see it in his movements. Grimple came at us from the opposite direction.

I recognized the weapons the villains were holding, of course—they'd been stolen from Zupan Manor—and I knew they were better than what Julianne and I had.

The Brothers Grin started toward us too, nightsticks swinging. The only sounds up on the ridge were the whines of the foxes and the muffled cries of Elias, who was kicking and fighting to free himself inside the Jeep.

I'd have to use my bad hand to fence, but that was the least of our worries. I swished the blade of my rapier through the air a few times, then squared up my stance.

"*En garde!*" Julianne and I said in unison.

I dove for Snidewater and she went after the Brothers Grin. We spun away from each other—feinting, dodging, then attacking with blazing speed.

When our enemies fell back, we rotated, as if we were dancing.

Now it was my turn to fight Snidewater and Deadly Dirk. They tried coming at me at once, and I beat them back in double time. When Dirk slashed at my legs, I jumped over his sword. When Snidewater swung at my head, I ducked it.

Three times, I pressed the Brothers Grin to the edge of the cliff—but each time they swung their nightsticks like battering rams and made it back onto solid ground.

Snidewater and Grimple were both fencers. Snidewater was technical—waiting for even the tiniest hole in my guard. Grimple was a beast, giving loud grunts each time he attacked, swinging his sword wildly. Still, they both had cuts on their arms before the first stage of the battle was over.

I glanced at Ronald. Even with a hurt shoulder, the Brothers Grin were no match for him.

Then it happened.

FACT: The Jeep started rolling toward the cliff.

"*Sato!*" I yelled.

I spun away from the Brothers Grin and threw her my sword. She snatched it out of the air, and in an instant she had both blades whirling.

I dove for the Jeep, just twenty feet from the towering cliffs of Hode Point, and grabbed the driver's door. Flinging the door open with my left hand almost made me collapse in pain, but I slid into the driver's seat, just in time.

I slammed the car into park and jerked the emergency brake as hard as I possibly could. Elias screamed through the handkerchief tied around his mouth. Rocks and gravel skidded under our tires. The Jeep started grinding to a halt.

Then—

The front two wheels of the Jeep slid over the cliff. The tail end tilted and the entire vehicle rocked back and forth. It was perched right on the ledge.

The Brothers Grin charged from the right. Snidewater and Deadly Dirk came at me from the left. I attacked them all with every trick I knew.

I slashed at their hands.

I jabbed at their legs.

I lunged left, then right.

But they just kept coming.

I untied Elias and tore the kerchief off his mouth. Neither of us dared to speak. We hardly dared to breathe. Slowly, so slowly, we began to inch toward the back hatch, sliding over the second row of seats like two salamanders.

"I accidentally kicked the parking brake with my foot," Elias whispered.

I didn't answer. My breathing was racing out of control, and I knew that any wrong move meant death.

When we finally made it to the trunk, I creaked open the back gate. We shuffled forward a little more—with the Jeep tottering on the ledge and Julianne fighting to keep our enemies away. I motioned to Elias, and we jumped off the bumper onto solid ground.

No sooner had we landed than the Jeep tipped back the other way and went over the cliff. Seconds later, we heard it hit the water with a massive splash.

Julianne's swords rang out in a sort of musical rhythm. My skin rippled with goose bumps. Each strike of my adventure partner's blades seemed to scream, *Not today, rapscallions!*

The second the Jeep went off the cliff, a strange thing happened. By the light of the moon, I could see the pack of fennec foxes start to slink closer. Without the motor to scare them away, there was nothing keeping them back.

Snidewater, Deadly Dirk, and the Brothers Grin formed a half circle around us. I passed Ronald back his sword and he whipped it through the air so fast it whistled. Elias pulled his slingshot out of his pocket, snatched up a rock from the edge of the cliff, and drew it back.

We were locked in a standoff. Four of them. Three of us. And five hundred foxes slowly closing in. But I still felt like we had the advantage. Or at least I did . . . until Dirk Grimple started to laugh.

"What's so funny, Dirk?" Snidewater asked.

Bill Grin's mustache twitched. Jake mopped streams of sweat from the side of his face.

"Boss," Grimple said, "I have to tell you something."

Snidewater didn't answer, just crouched low, with the point of his sword hovering a few inches from mine. Our enemies couldn't see it, but all this time, the massive group of fennec foxes was tightening around us.

"It's good news," Grimple went on. "I think you'll like it."

"*Spit it out!*" Snidewater said.

Grimple reached inside his coat. "I still have one Roman candle left."

47

Sato's Siege!

My friends and I watched helplessly as Dirk Grimple reached into his coat with his free hand and drew out a long firework that looked like a wand. Next, he handed his sword to his boss and dug in his pocket. A second later, he pulled his hand back out with his fingers wrapped around a lighter in a silver case. He snapped it open with his thumb and a little tongue of flame danced in the wind.

"Friends, we have to do something," Ronald said. "If Grimple fires that at us . . ."

The villains could all hear us, of course, but it didn't matter now. Ronald was right. We had to act.

"What do we do?" Elias said.

Ronald held his blade in his good hand, wincing from the pain. "We have to charge. Right toward the foxes."

His words surprised our enemies, and they looked behind them, finally noticing the scores of fennec foxes gathering nearby. Bill Grin gave a sad whimper at the sight of them.

"Light the wick," Snidewater said. "Shoot them with the Roman candle, and we'll push the three of them right off the cliff. Then I will be the leader of the Liars' Club."

Grimple went to light the wick. As he did, I had the flash of an idea. I could actually feel my lips curving into a smile.

"Ronald," I said, "The Danger Gang trusts each other's hunches, right?"

The words caught him off guard and he looked at me. At the same moment, I smelled sulfur in the air. The wick of the Roman candle was burning.

He gave me a smirk. "Of course. It's part of our code."

Julianne dropped her sword on the ground and moved behind me. Her heels must've been right on the edge of the cliff. She rummaged through the satchel slung across my back, then I heard the peeling of the top of a tin can.

"*Get down!*" Julianne yelled, just as a burst of blue sparks showered from the end of Dirk Grimple's Roman candle. Elias and I dropped to the ground as Julianne threw anchovies from the last two cans at our enemies.

All four of the rogues got a handful of oily fish right across their faces.

Dirk Grimple dropped the Roman candle and it rolled off the edge of the cliff. Then there was a moment of silence on the ridge.

"Maybe I was wron—"

But before Julianne could get the word out, we heard them, tearing toward us. Yowling in the moonlight.

FACT: The fennec foxes had caught the scent of the anchovies. And they looked hungry.

"*Now run!*" Julianne yelled.

"To the tunnel!" Elias called. "The Brothers Grin left it open."

I was just a foot away from Snidewater but he was still blinded by anchovies. I dropped to my knees and slashed at his pant leg—on the same side where he'd tucked the Brasher Doubloon back on the Serpent of the Mist. Then I spun away, dodging between the Brothers Grin. We were ten steps from the tunnel when we heard Snidewater scream. We all turned.

He had a fox on his coat, snarling, trying to lap up the anchovies as they slid down his neck. The foxes closed in fast now—so thick you couldn't see the ground around them. Dirk Grimple, Jake and Bill Grin, and the devilish Snidewater were all backed up to the edge of the cliff.

"*I HATE these foxes!*" Bill Grin bellowed. He turned toward the water and jumped.

Jake and Deadly Dirk leaped right after him.

Snidewater wiped his face and looked over his shoulder at us. He had foxes chewing on his pant legs and biting at his hands. It was clear that he had only one choice.

"I'll get my revenge!" he screamed. "You haven't heard the last of me. I'm your archenemyyyy

YYYYYY

YYYYY

YYY

Y

Y

Y

Y

Y

Y

Y

The three of us stood at the door to the tunnel, speechless. It was quiet for a second, then the silence was broken by the sound of a blaring air horn. The foxes scattered. Suraya came into view from the direction of Hode House. She was on foot, racing toward the cliff, sounding the air horn every few steps. It seemed to scare the foxes every bit as much as a car motor did.

A second later, we saw my parents, Jeeves, Isa, Mr. Sato, and Josh hurrying after her. We raced to meet them along Hode Point. Without the lights of the Jeep, it was too dark to see, but we could hear the rogues screaming in agony. I stooped down and picked up the Brasher Doubloon. It had fallen to the dirt when I sliced Snidewater's pocket— just as I'd hoped. I passed it to my father with a smile.

"Well, Jeeves," I said, as my beloved butler approached. "It turns out you *can* survive jumping off that cliff."

Jeeves gave me a wry smirk. "It doesn't sound like much fun though."

We could hear the men moaning in pain two hundred feet below. Finally, the engine of a boat roared to life and the villains puttered off into the dark night. Defeated by the Danger Gang.

Before they could get a hundred yards, the purple horizon glowed red. A colossal boom came to us three seconds later. The Serpent of the Mist was up in flames. Sparks flew in all directions.

We stood side by side by side watching the last of the fireworks blaze their paths across the horizon while the Serpent dropped into the abyss. Then the others turned and stepped inside the tunnels, leaving Julianne, Jeeves, and me alone for the briefest moment.

"See, Ronald," my beloved butler said with a smile, "seems like you had nothing to worry about."

I looked at him, confused. The pain in my shoulder made me woozy. "I'm not sure what you—"

"Rule number seven on your father's list for avoiding the second-adventure slump," he said, "'finish with an explosion.' Well there you go."

Julianne braced me as we walked to the tunnel door. "All in all, not a bad second adventure, right?"

I looked back at the sinking Serpent. A sparrow whizzed past the cliffs, chirping to announce the coming sunrise. My friends stepped into the tunnels and I followed, closing the door with my good arm.

"No," I said, "not bad at all."

EPILOGUE

The Second Movie Premiere!

Three weeks after the battle of Hode Point, we were back at Capstone Island. Most of the FIB had escaped the police but the island itself had been seized. People had gotten interested in it again after our exploits made the papers and there was even talk of turning it into an official nature preserve.

In the meantime, Josh Brigand convinced Capstone Motion Pictures to renovate the old theater so he could debut a new cut of *Buccaneers of the South Seas*. He'd promised his critics that his new version of the film would have far less banter with his parrot and far more scenes with Queen Esmeralda. He'd even done reshoots, adding a scene where she rescues him at the beginning of the movie's third act.

After reading all the details of Josh's kidnapping at the hands of the FIB, everyone back in Bay City tried to get tickets to the second premiere. A whole fleet of seaplanes and

yachts buzzed over from the mainland. Their passengers stepped ashore in tuxedos and ball gowns, peering left and right in hopes of spotting the fennec foxes that they'd heard so much about.

My parents and I arrived in the Zupan family seaplane. Before the movie, we walked through the tunnels, for a picnic at Hode Point—we talked for hours about the best ways to escape a charging rhinoceros, where to find old pirate coins after a hurricane, and what the best method might be for recovering the Zupan family artifacts from the bottom of the ocean. Since it wouldn't take too long to get the relics from the sunken iceberg, I suggested calling it an "add-on exploit."

After dessert, my parents made me a promise. No matter how busy things got—with me braving the dangers of public school and them trying to track down Snidewater and his crew—we'd always save Friday-night dinners just for the three of us and our closest friends.

"It's a dashing plan," I said, then paused. "One question, though." My parents nodded for me to go on. "Why didn't you tell me anything about your investigation of the FIB? I thought after defeating Zeetan Z, you'd let me help."

They looked at each other, then back to me.

"We were embarrassed," my father admitted with a shrug. "We thought you'd think less of us—first getting caught by pirates in Borneo, then getting stumped by the FIB. We had no idea where their hideout was."

My mother nodded in agreement. We'd been searching for days and days . . . only to end up in a daze."

I looked at my mom first, then my dad. "Jeeves says, 'Sometimes, no matter how much effort you give, things just won't work out. That's when you need people to help you.'"

Helen smiled. "Jeeves said that, huh?"

I nodded.

My father rose to his feet and helped my mother and me up. "That's very good advice," he said, glancing at his watch. It was time to start walking back through the tunnels, and there was a pack of fennec foxes eyeing us a little too eagerly. "I promise: from now on, no more secrets about the FIB or the Liars' Club, agreed?"

We shook on it, then both parents put their arms across my shoulders and we walked toward the tunnels. By the time we made it back to the theater, up the aisle, and outside to meet our friends, everyone was already there. Almost.

Mr. Sato and Elexander were chatting with Josh, Julianne and Isa were over in a corner practicing swordfighting techniques, and Suraya and Elias were leaning up against a brand-new fence they'd built. As I approached, Julianne caught my eye and we pulled Elias aside.

With the adults out of earshot, Julianne handed him a gift we'd bought and wrapped in crepe paper.

"For me?" he asked.

We nodded in unison.

Elias tore it open and flipped the pages. "It's . . . it's . . ."

"Your first adventure journal," I said.

"Welcome to the Danger Gang," Julianne added. "We also got you this fountain pen and a pot of India ink."

Elias beamed and raced back to the group to show his mom. A woman in a long red coat walked around the front of the theater, ringing a bell to signal that the movie was about to start. As everyone else filed inside, my eyes caught on Jeeves, strolling in our direction. The others noticed him too. He was dressed in a tuxedo with a white carnation in his lapel.

"Jeeves," I said, "I thought you weren't the movie-going type. That's what you told us back in Bay City."

"I'm not," the butler said, grinning shyly. "But I do . . . make some exceptions."

I looked at Julianne, who motioned to Delenda's crabbing boat tied up to the seawall. The captain stepped out of her cabin. Her dress was the color of midnight and shimmered like it had been covered with stardust.

Jeeves's face started to turn pink as she approached.

"Ready, Tom?" she asked, a little unsteady in high heels.

The good butler offered her his arm. "Absolutely."

The rest of us followed Jeeves and Delenda into the theater, where Josh had two entire rows reserved for us. As the credits started to roll, I tapped Jeeves on the shoulder. He turned around to find Julianne, Elias, and me all leaning forward in our seats.

"Danger Gang members," I said in a hushed voice, "I've been thinking a lot about our third adventure . . ."

Ronald trailed off and I looked over at him. He flipped open his adventure journal to reveal a map that he'd drawn himself. It showed Alejandro Selkirk Island, off the coast of Chile.

Looking at the map, I had to bat back tears. Ronald had studied the ocean currents and marked it with guesses about where my parents' ship had wrecked when I was just a baby.

"Julianne has a music box aboard a sunken ship somewhere near this island," he said to Jeeves and Elias. "We have to help her find it."

I looked at him. "That's the whole adventure? We don't need to do anything else to avoid a . . . third adventure fallout or something?"

"Nope," he said

The others turned toward the movie, but Ronald was still looking at me. Finally he grinned. "I mean, if we *happen* to discover forgotten ruins it would be great, but . . . how does this sound for a third adventure? It's your choice as much as mine."

I smiled at him. "It's perfect."

The movie was starting, so we didn't say anything else, but that moment—sitting with my friends, getting to watch a movie starring Josh and Isa, with another adventure on the horizon—seems like a perfect place to end this story.

Of course, I know how Ronald likes to have the last word, so he'll probably jump in one last time.

No I won't. I don't need the last word this time.

FACT: Your ending was perfect.

You sure?

Indeed!

But you keep cutting in!

You haven't written "the end" yet.

Okay, "the end!"

Excellent!

Ahem.

Oops, give me one more try!

THE END.

Acknowledgments

If Francisco Zupan were giving us all advice he'd say, "Saying thank you to your fellow expedition members is a vital part of the adventurer's toolkit, just like a mosquito net." If it were Helen dishing out the words of wisdom it might be, "It's great to be grateful and is sure to grate on people if you're not."

I agree with them, so here goes: a list of people I want to say thank you to, for helping with this book.

1. You. For reading. For liking Ronald, Julianne, Elias, Jeeves, Isa, the Zupans, Delenda, Mr. Sato, Elexander Davidson, Jolly Briphead—er . . . I mean Josh Brigand—and the whole team. For rooting for them when villains attack and laughing with them when they're finally safe again.

2. To my family. To my mom, who loves stories more than anyone I know, and my dad, who passed away but guides me literally every day. To my two incredible sisters, Gina and Anna, who make me want to be a better human (they're both so smart!). To every member of my beloved Parker familia— being born related to all of you is far better than being born

the Prince of Monaco. And to my in-laws Nazy and Ali who make time for me to write by helping take care of my son (and buy copies of my books even though I'd gladly give them copies for free!).

3. To my friends (both writers and nonwriters): the Great Jah-Coby, Surfer Sam, M-Dubs & R-H, Mr. V, Joey the Irish, Mikey McG, Kev-Dog, Jarret the Freshmaker, Studio Steve V . . . this list could go for ages.

4. To Arree Chung, whose expert illustrations helped this world come alive.

5. To the Bloomsbury Team, starting with my brilliant editor, Mary Kate Castellani, power publicist Courtney Griffin, and the very wise, very generous team of Cindy Loh, Claire Stetzer, Emily Ritter, Oona Patrick, Jeanette Levy, Melissa Kavonic, Liz Byer, Amanda Bartlett, Nick Sweeney, Donna Mark, Erica Barmash, Phoebe Dyer, Lizzy Mason, Erica Loberg, Beth Eller, Brittany Mitchell, and Nicholas Church.

6. To the Pippin Properties Team, who have been kind to me since day one, especially my fierce, always positive super-agent Sara Crowe.

7. To my partner, Nikta, who . . . put it this way: when she saw a display of my first book in stores, she started crying from happiness. That's the sort of person every writer needs and the sort I'm so lucky to spend my days with.

8. To our son, Julien River, for making literally every moment a thrilling escapade full of intrigue and excitement.

9. Finally (I could go on for pages and pages, but you might get bored and I'd run out of room), I want to thank the Danger Gang, the Liars' Club, and the FIB. In my life, I've been lucky enough to have tons of fun all over the world, but never have I had so much fun as spending long afternoons with them, writing stories of pirates and smugglers. I will miss them immeasurably.

Thanks and thanks and thanks and thanks and thanks some more. Knowing all the people thanked here is the greatest adventure I could imagine.